The Unnamed Town

BOOK TWO OF THE AWAKENING WARS

WILLIAM H. NELSON

Infinite Worlds Publishing
Copyright © William H. Nelson 2021

ISBN: 978-1-7344642-2-1 (paperback)
ISBN: 978-1-7344642-3-8 (ebook)

Front Cover Art and Design: William H. Nelson

Other Books by William H. Nelson

Nathrotep

Within the Range of Reanimation
(Book One of the Awakening Wars)

Acknowledgements

First off I would like to thank Lisa Paschke, the love of my life and my partner in everything. Without her continued encouragement and support, I wouldn't be able to get these stories written and published. I would also like to thank my language consultants, Maryland Aviuk Panigeo and her husband Ronald Qiilu Panigeo. They were kind enough to once more translate the necessary dialogue into readable Iñupiaq. Without their input, I wouldn't be able to create such compelling and believable characters. And a huge thanks goes out to Eris Hyrkas, the super cool cousin that I didn't know I had until a few months ago. She graciously offered to do the preliminary editing, which is a service that I am eternally grateful for. In addition to all of those folks, I'd also like to give a shout out to everyone over at EbookPbook. They worked incredibly hard at getting the formatting, cover art, and final edits completed, and I appreciate all they have done to prepare this novella for publication. To everyone else who's ever taken the time to peruse my work, I give you my most humblest of thanks. Without you readers the worlds I'm creating would never come to life in any meaningful way. Thank you all so very much.

Prologue

Director Anne Wilkenson

"Here are the files that you requested, *Director*," he announced, his voice dripping with sarcasm as he slid the folders onto my desk. Then, with an air of barely contained hostility, he strode from the office without so much as a "by your leave."

Gritting my teeth, I dragged the pile of reports closer, managing to murmur a hasty "thank you" as the agent disappeared around the corner of the doorframe. This was not how this was supposed to be. This should have been my big promotion, the highlight of my career that I'd been working toward my entire life. But, instead, it was all just complete bullshit. I'd wanted this position since I'd joined the Extraterrestrial Defense Agency, but not this way, not by default like this. The rest of my team, predominately male, had always had a bit of a problem with me. My higher scores at the Academy, my better marksmanship, my rapid rise through the ranks, all of it seemed to threaten them like a challenge to their questionable superiority. But I'd been making progress, winning them over gradually, had even formed a few solid friendships among the ranks. Yet now that the director and the deputy director had both been killed in those fucking mountains, I'd been ordered to assume control over this branch of our organization simply because I was the highest-ranking member left alive. Originally, my plan had always been to work my way up to this position, earning the title based on merit, while attempting to gain the trust and respect of the rest of my colleagues along the way. Only that opportunity was forever lost to me now, all just becoming a pipe dream as I was catapulted into the directorship by that damned invasive species we'd discovered in the mountains of northern Alaska. Leaning back in my chair, I stared out the window, watching the fall leaves swirl around the busy downtown streets of Anchorage as I brooded on my predicament.

We'd taken over the FBI headquarters on Sixth Avenue right after our near defeat by that strange race of otherworldly creatures who'd attacked us up in the Brooks Range. In regard to that isolated location, I still had cleanup crews sweeping the area, and the official story going out was that a previously quiescent volcano had erupted unexpectedly. The whole place was quarantined, while the remaining members of my team dissected some of the dead extraterrestrials we'd salvaged after the battle. In addition to that, I also had workers digging into the surrounding hillside in an attempt to see where these things had come from to begin with. Yet, after so much heat and explosive destruction, my men had found very little of use to us so far.

It was infuriating that most of the insect-like beings had gotten away, but even now I had other agents assigned to tracking them down and finding out where the hell they'd got off to. A great many had flown up into the sky and then right out into the depths of space, or so I'd been told by our contacts at NASA. Others had scurried off into the surrounding wilderness, disappearing into the dense mountain woodlands without a trace. Now there was no time left to mourn our losses, no chance for me to work at getting the rest of the agents to support my unexpected rise to the position of director. I had to take up the reins of leadership and then whip this investigation into shape without any of the niceties I might once have employed to win over the rest of my team. The brutal fact of the matter was that we had to find out what we were up against, and fast, before the entire planet was overrun by forces that we, as of now, knew next to nothing about.

It was a lot to deal with, but that was the whole reason why departments like my own had been created in the first place. The Extraterrestrial Defense Agency was there for just such a contingency. We were the first and last line of defense the planet had against the threat of an alien invasion. Most of the time we were the butt of sarcastic jokes but, to be honest, this wasn't our first rodeo, even though it was, by far, the most fucktangular assignment that I'd ever taken part in.

Sighing, I ran my hand through the short, spiky hair covering my scalp, turning my attention back to the files on my desk. It was imperative that we find the missing hunters, those two men who'd absconded with the helicopter my team had originally commandeered from the Kotzebue airport. They'd been at the scene, had been standing next to one of the alien devices that even now the tech department was still salivating over, although, as of yet, they had no clue as to what its purpose was. What were those men doing out there and why? I'd discovered their identities easily enough. After my team had located the pilot they'd left with, he'd spilled his beans without any reservations.

It would seem that these boys were from a small native community just north of the containment site, one that now claimed to have no idea where they'd got off to or when they'd be returning. After some routine digging around, my agents had found out they'd first stopped off at their village to warn them of the danger posed by the invasive species before fleeing in the helicopter back to Kotzebue. After that, they'd immediately booked passage on a commercial flight out of Ralph Wien Memorial Airport heading toward Anchorage. However, they'd fallen off the radar right after disembarking the plane, and I still had men out searching for them. They'd eluded me for now, but it was only a matter of time. I'd find them, and when I did, those bastards would answer my questions, oh yes, they most certainly would.

I was sure that once we brought them in, they'd be able to shed some more light on what had been going on inside the artificial mountain that had mysteriously appeared in the Brooks Range. It had risen up during a sizable earthquake and then inexplicably turned into a fiery crater just before my team arrived at the scene. The race of beings that created this massive structure, these peculiar lifeforms with their advanced technology and abilities to travel through space without a ship, had to be a known threat, at least within the top-ranking echelons of our own government.

The trouble was that my agency was purposely split into many smaller branches that operated independently of each other. Designed as separate, insulated units, we were kept isolated from the other teams in the interests of national security. Although all of us were required to report to the same higher authority, our superiors only distributed enough information for each unit to do their jobs effectively with little or no supervision. We were the government's elite ground troops and operated under the strictest of secrecy, but it was up to the top brass to make all the tough calls and hard decisions before giving us our orders accordingly. For all I knew, these beings could be just another known interstellar threat in the growing pantheon of creatures not native to this planet that my superiors were already dealing with. I'd just have to wait and see what information they deigned to give me after they received my next report. For now, I was simply ordered to accumulate more intel and finish the job that my team had been sent out here to do.

And for that, I needed to find these two native hunters. Pronto.

Leaning back in the chair once more, I stared out the window, watching the people walking by as I contemplated my options. There had to be some way I could get control of the situation and wring the respect I so richly deserved from my disgruntled teammates before they mutinied and fucked me straight up the ass. I was positive that once I had things running smoothly, everyone would agree I was the right choice to head up this department, no matter how the position had come to me.

But until then, I'd simply have to win them over as I went along. Then, after gaining their trust and support, I'd be able to show those rat-bastard naysayers a thing or two about what made Anne Wilkenson tick all right. And I was going to give it to them all with both barrels—they didn't know who the fuck they were messing with. Yet. But they'd find out soon enough, and by then I would have either earned their respect, or at least obtained their unequivocal cooperation.

As the leaves floated down outside, I planned the next moves I'd make to ensure all of this came to fruition in the way I envisioned it, my thoughts correlating and refining my ideas as I focused on how I could best obtain the bright future ahead that I saw for myself.

And one thing above all else was painfully clear: I could not allow myself to fail.

1

Gillam

The town had that deserted, ghost-ridden feeling, like a catastrophe had struck at some point in the far distant past, causing the folk who once lived here to either all die horrible deaths or to run screaming for the hills. Driving along the trash-blown streets, I couldn't help but wonder what had happened here. It was strange, but there were no indications of it on any maps that we'd found, and the GPS wasn't getting a signal this far away from the nearest cell towers. We were in an area that time had forgotten about, a town on the edge of nowhere, populated by the shadows of people no longer truly alive.

As we drove through it, we passed dozens of deserted homes and buildings with bleak, darkened windows, like the empty sockets on a crow-pecked skull. They all appeared to have been devastated by some unknown calamity, their walls sagging and roofs collapsed, with glass and other leftover debris choking their overgrown lots. I was able to spot a few inhabitants still lurking in the alleyways, but they all had a lean and foreboding look about them. More than that, they exhibited a certain skittishness, an unwillingness to be seen that was revealed in how they cringed away from my curious gaze, their eyes never meeting my own for more than a few seconds before they scuttled away. It was downright unnerving.

I glanced aside at Tunuhun where he sat in the passenger seat of the car we'd borrowed from one of my late uncle's private safe houses. He seemed calm, cool, and collected as always, like this was just another hunt out on the ice flows where we'd grown up together. The man was unflappable, and I tried my best to emulate him, to stop my nervous energy from getting the best of me. But given our current situation, it was difficult to maintain a similar sense of serenity.

We were here seeking a man that my uncle had once known, someone my aunt had told us about when we'd met with her in Anchorage after fleeing the site of the alien hive we'd discovered in the Brooks Range. She provided a great deal of assistance in our quest to translate the map tile fragment, and I knew I would never be able to repay her for all that she'd done. Perhaps stopping these repellent creatures from invading our world would be enough to show my gratitude, but I had my doubts that we could even accomplish that much. Facing a sentient race that was so far beyond us in both evolution and technology while also evading the government forces that were persistently dogging our heels seemed to be a fever dream from which I could not awaken. But there was no way I'd give up now. Something inside me drove me onward, something more than just the need to avenge our friend who'd been dissected by the horrific, insectile creatures we'd faced in that ancient arctic base.

I shifted in the driver's seat as a coldness spread outward from my belly, causing my limbs to tremble ever so slightly. The sensory input from that other lifeform we'd encountered, the barrel-shaped, star-headed abomination who'd been held captive by those malevolent insectoids, was still woven through my thoughts. Its persuasive influence overloaded my mind at odd times with images and information that I strove to keep from haunting my every waking moment. It was an ongoing internal battle, and one that I hoped would not hinder us in the next few days as we tried to obtain the information we needed.

Without my aunt's help, we would never have made it even this far. Thinking back, I once again remembered all she'd done for us when we met with her a few days ago.

After the helicopter had taken us to our small village so we could warn them, I'd been able to persuade the pilot to give us a lift back to his home base at the Kotzebue Airport. Once there, I'd borrowed a cell phone from a stranger waiting in line at the ticket counter to briefly speak with my aunt, and she'd agreed to meet with us. Because of this call, a car was waiting after we'd touched down in Anchorage, and the driver had taken us directly to her mansion up in Hillside East. It was one of the many estates that she now owned after my uncle had passed away, but one that she made her primary residence to be closer to our shared tribal community.

My late uncle had been an archaeologist and a great explorer, a man who had no trouble selling off the rich findings from his adventures in order to better himself and fund even more extravagant expeditions around the globe. After his untimely death, all of his holdings had transferred to my aunt, making her one of the wealthiest women currently residing within the United States. My uncle's penchant for finding ancient artifacts and rediscovering lost civilizations had been both a boon and a hardship for them, as many people had condemned him for his constant plundering of newly discovered historical sites. However, since he'd been the one funding his own excursions and often gave back to the scientific community, his explorations, although met with much scrutiny and denouncement, were mostly left unobstructed.

Now that he was gone, my aunt managed the vast fortune he had accumulated in his long lifetime with a shrewd and uncompromising business acumen that kept the profits rolling in from their many diversified investments. I learned much from her in my youth, and as a favored nephew had benefited greatly from my uncle's benevolent bequeathments to my extensive college education. As we pulled into the driveway of her sprawling hillside manor, I was both relieved and somewhat nervous. How much could I tell her about what had befallen us? Would she offer to assist us any more than she had already done, or would we be sent packing, straight back into the arms of the government agents who even now sought to capture and interrogate us? Squaring my shoulders, I decided that I would be as honest as possible with her. After all, she was my beloved aunt—surely she would at least offer us her guidance and wisdom.

She was a strong-willed individual, and in great physical health for someone who was sixty-five years old, so I wasn't surprised to find her waiting for us on the huge wraparound porch of the well-lit, three-story home. With a smile that crinkled up her face so much that it almost hid the glint in her dark, inquisitive eyes, she watched as the chauffeur opened the door for us so we could disembark from the backseat of the sleek Mercedes Maybach S-Class. I noticed that she was dressed conservatively as always, with a dark pair of slacks and a loose, neutral-colored blouse. In addition to that, a multicolored scarf was knotted around her neck to hide the scar she had from an old surgery, and her only concession to the cold of late August was the knitted shawl she'd placed about her shoulders against the chill. I have to admit that upon seeing her I felt an immense surge of relief. With her help, I had hope that we might just have a chance in this mad quest we were determined to embark upon.

As soon as we exited the vehicle, she ambled down the stairs, enfolding me in a warm embrace. "It is good to see you, Gill," she exclaimed, her accent still a bit thick with the influence of our native tongue. Then, holding me out at arm's length, she glanced over at Tunuhun. "Qanugitpiñ, Tunny!"

Tunuhun smiled at her use of our childhood nicknames and of her welcoming him in our own language, ducking his head to hide his embarrassment. We were still dressed in our filthy, torn clothing from the expedition to that great Euclidean hive up in the Brooks Range. There'd been no time to buy new outfits or change during our escape from the pursuing EDA agents. Looking us over, she *tsked* between her teeth and then gave orders to her staff, a couple of household assistants that had come out onto the porch behind her when we'd arrived. In short order, we were escorted to the grand living room and then settled into comfortable chairs with steaming mugs of rich, dark coffee in our hands. Without further preamble, she took a seat across from us and then studied us with a great deal of concern crossing her blunt features.

"As much as I would like it to be," she began, "I realize that this isn't just a social call. What have you two boys gotten yourselves into this time?"

I didn't know where to start. To give myself some time to collect my thoughts, I glanced around the huge living area, once again marveling at the exotic wood paneling, the floor-to-ceiling windows overlooking the city, and the mixture of artifacts and knick-knacks that decorated the entire space. In their time together, my aunt and uncle had shared an abundance of similar tastes, but he'd always bowed to her fancies in the decorating of their many homes, especially this one. So it was that there were butterfly displays mounted on the walls next to cartography charts, carved, wooded owls on shelves next to ancient tribal pottery, and a variety of other cultural or purely decorative items arranged among his own more antediluvian collectibles. The effect was rather stunning, if a trifle eclectic, and I let myself be soothed by the familiarity of this room that I knew so well from my youth. After a few moments, I let my eyes wander back to my aunt, who waited patiently for me to explain. Taking a deep breath, I began, holding nothing back.

I told her of the village and its need to find answers once the strange mountain had thrust itself up from the ground in the middle of the Brooks Range, of our journey there, the three of us, including Opeim, who'd died a horrible death within that foul place. Describing the interior of the nest of hibernating extraterrestrial life, I detailed what we'd found—the map room, the dissection areas, and the gigantic communications globe. She gasped aloud as I spoke of our near fatal experience in trying to vacate that vast central chamber, and the alien thoughts that flooded my mind from the barrel-shaped beings whom we'd freed from their age-old captivity. Then I told her of how those very same creatures had helped us indirectly by attacking their ancient foes, and of our explosive ejection from that mountainous base when the pod that Tunuhun had sealed us into had been blasted clear during the resulting eruption of their accursed technology. Through it all, she listened with a grave expression, never once interrupting, and not seeming surprised at all to hear about the things I was telling her.

When I was done, she folded her hands in her lap, her piercing eyes gazing at me from out of the wrinkled folds of her age-weathered face. "You know," she began, "your uncle tried to keep me out of his most recent explorations. I think he thought it would help to ensure my safety. But I am not some delicate flower, some nitwit woman with no courage nor brain to speak of! I am of *our* tribe, and we have always been strong in mind and spirit. I knew of his discoveries, and a lot of the things that you're telling me now are very similar to some of the hidden lore he was stumbling across over the last several years of his life. There are many things going on in this world right now—secret cults, the rediscovery of lost civilizations, beings of indescribable power and hunger on the rise. These creatures you speak of, they may very well have been a part of what he was getting mixed up in there toward the end, things that I think might have attributed to his death." Her eyes grew cold, and I felt a chill run through me as she sat up straighter on the divan across from us. "I will help you, and through you, I will strike back at the ones who've taken him from me."

It was as if I were seeing her for the very first time, a new understanding blooming within the depths of my mind. She'd always been a strong influence in my life, from days long ago when I was but a child, and she'd helped me with my lessons or taught me things that a young, inquisitive native boy often yearned to know about the wide world around him. But now I saw her in a very different light. Her strength of will and sense of conviction shone from her like a testament to our people's indomitable spirit.

Seeing it made me recall that our tribe was made up of subsistence hunters with a rich heritage going back thousands of years. It was a history steeped with tradition, a hard way of life, but a very fulfilling one. I'd never considered how others might perceive us until now. What we did regularly to survive, some might view as extreme. But even though hunting the animals and sea life of the arctic regions was challenging and sometimes difficult, for us it was just simply what we were born to do. Looking back at it now, I saw that our lifestyle and traditions had uniquely prepared us to face this alien invasion, this upwelling of occult madness and otherworldly threats. Our minds and bodies were used to overcoming daily challenges that most people would find incapacitating.

And yet, we excelled at it.

Glancing around the room once more, I saw that a lot of the items on display held occult significance that I hadn't at first realized, while still others were wholly tribal in nature, a mixture of my aunt and uncle's passions collected together in one place over the many years of their marriage. Here was a great source of inspiration, and also a window into my aunt's soul that I had not fully appreciated before. The pride within me swelled as my eyes stole back to fixate upon her, seeing clearly her steadfast determination to help us in any way that she could.

"I appreciate your offer," I said, "but we don't even know where to begin." Showing her the engraved piece of stone that I now held in my hand, I gave a slight shrug of one shoulder and then continued, "This fragment that we've taken from the archive room inside that reawakened base is indecipherable, leastwise to us. For now. As far as I can tell, it's part of a map, something that may lead us where we need to go, perhaps even to someplace where we can find the means to stop these beings from conquering the Earth."

Leaning forward, she gazed at the artifact with her hands still folded in her ample lap. "It seems that you boys have a mystery to untangle," she said. Then, reaching over to a side table, she picked up an electronic device half the size of a small laptop. "This is Edward's private tablet. It has all of his notes, his findings, access to his offshore accounts, and the locations of safe houses around the globe. You'll find it all in here, and I'll give you the encryption codes to access it." Handing it across to me, she then leaned back and went on. "I'll also give you the startup funds you'll need and provide further help, as I can. Edward had many hidden places where he kept a great deal of his more sensitive materials. He didn't trust the government, and set up dummy corporations to generate the cash flow needed to facilitate the more clandestine aspects of his lifestyle. With this device, you'll be able to get into these hidden places and resupply as needed. Maybe you'll even discover some clues to help you along the way. I can't tell you much about what he was into; I once promised him I would never meddle too deeply into his affairs. But now that he's passed on—well, I never promised him I wouldn't look into these things after he was gone."

I was taken aback by her generosity, but knew that it was all for a good cause. If we didn't stop this madness, then who would? The government? Unlikely. They had their hands full with world affairs. Besides, nobody was going to believe us if we tried to warn them about what we'd found. Even those agents that attempted to detain us would most likely have no idea what was now at stake. No, it would be better for us to try and figure things out for ourselves. At least for the time being.

"What you're doing for us goes well beyond all our expectations," I said, "but we still don't even know where to begin. We need help, someone that can read these pictographs, decipher what this fragment means, somebody who's into all this other metaphysical stuff you've mentioned. What about some of Edward's business associates? Can any of them be trusted?"

She thought for a moment, but then shook her head. "Sadly, he kept most of the more dangerous manuscripts and artifacts out of his main buyer's hands. They were too dangerous, in his estimation, to have floating around in someone's private collection of forbidden knowledge. There are some facilities that might be of help to you—universities and other places of learning that have purchased items from him over the years. But you'll never be able to get into those places without his help. They have high levels of security to protect their assets, and the items that they've stored in these collections are not open for public viewing. Plus, those Feds you told me about will be hot on your trail very soon and they'd easily track you to any one of these institutions." Pursing her lips, she squinted her eyes, looking up at the ceiling while she thought things through. "There is one man," she finally said, rather reluctantly. "He's someone that your uncle sold to often, but he also placed items into this man's care to safeguard them as well. I never knew the reason why—the man is a complete lunatic, if you ask me. But he does know a great deal about the things your uncle was getting himself into during the last thirty or so years of his life."

I knew it wouldn't be an ideal solution, but I figured that any help right now would be better than nothing at all. "Where can we find this man?" I asked her.

"He lives in a small community that no longer exists," she replied. "It was a border town in Arizona that had a history of horrible things happening, or so I was told. I guess that's why it was taken off the map once things got too bad and most of the townsfolk moved away. Now you'll only be able to find it by using the tablet. But we'll start off by sending you to an acquaintance of mine who runs a shipping service here in town. He can get you out of Anchorage without anyone knowing, and you'll be able to pick up a vehicle at one of Edward's private safe houses when you arrive in Washington. If we do it this way, those agents will have a more difficult time in tracking you down. And they'll probably be here soon, if what you've told me about them is true. You best be going before they catch up to you. When they get here, I'll stall them for as long as I possibly can."

Clutching the tablet to my breast, my eyes filled with tears of gratitude. "Thank you, Auntie," I managed around the huge lump in my throat, "we will never forget what you've done for us."

My thoughts came back to the present as I maneuvered around a burnt-out car sitting in the middle of the road. We'd shipped out of Anchorage that very night, traveling on a cargo ship headed for Tacoma. From there, we'd used my uncle's tablet to locate one of his many safe houses, which was filled with artifacts, clothing, and supplies, as well as a few random vehicles he'd stored there. Now we'd been driving a black Buick Regal GNX for over twenty-three hours and, after many false turns and backtracking, we'd finally found this mysterious location on the border of Arizona. It was a place that had been dead now for many years, a community with a dark and sinister past, if my uncle's notes were to be believed. And it was here that we'd find his erstwhile business partner, the man whom we hoped would provide answers to some of our most pressing questions and help us to decipher the map fragment we'd taken from the alien hive. I knew it was a pretty weak plan, but he was our only lead thus far in the investigation, and so we continued on our way, moving through this nameless, fate-ravaged area in an effort to locate a shop known only as "The Source."

As we drove down the desolate streets, the creeping uncertainty of our journey weighed heavily upon me. This place was filled with a pervasive sense of death and destruction, even now while the sun was still just edging toward the horizon. Once or twice, I caught myself glancing in the rearview mirror, my eyes drawn by movement, yet finding nothing actually there. At least nothing that I could see. The persistent sense of being watched or followed continued to plague me as we traveled along, sending my fight-or-flight impulse into overload. But, squaring my shoulders, I shrugged off the uncomfortable sensation, focusing on my route instead. We had to locate this business associate my uncle spoke of in his notes as a trusted friend. Perhaps he could help us translate the fragment we carried, but I still had my doubts. I was betting both of our lives on the hope of this one man's willing assistance, and indeed the lives of everyone else on the planet as well. I just hoped he would be worth our time.

Squinting at the road signs hanging haphazardly at every corner, I made my way toward the area shown on the tablet, the place where we'd supposedly find this master of forbidden knowledge and his collection of curiosities. It was a good thing my uncle had mapped out a route since we would never have found it otherwise. As we rounded a corner and drove down another shadowy lane, we passed by a decrepit-looking graveyard. Slowing the car, I gazed at the destruction residing within the desolate field of ancient tombstones and overgrown mausoleums.

At the center of this place of age-old interment was a jagged crater with shards of broken wood poking out of it. Perhaps there once had been a great mansion or even a mortuary resting on that plot of decimated land, yet now it had been totally destroyed by some cataclysmic event. Shudders rolled unexpectedly through my body as I felt the presence of the creature that rode my thoughts trying to break through again, an attempt that I forcibly denied, sweat breaking out on my forehead as I struggled against this renewed attack of alien consciousness. There was something here that it wanted me to be aware of. Was it trying to warn me, or yet again take over my body for its own vile purposes? I didn't know for sure, and I really didn't care to find out. Shaking off the feelings of impending doom, I barred the creature from my mind once more, driving past the plot of moldering grave sites while making for the other side of town, hoping to at last discover the whereabouts of my uncle's one-time partner.

In a cul-de-sac at the end of a dead-end street, we finally found it. Painted by the dying rays of the setting sun, I saw unusual structures surrounding a derelict building which sat alone on a small rise. Pumping the brakes, I gazed at the perplexing sight that rested before us in the semi-darkness of approaching twilight. It was as if a madman had cobbled together barriers out of clapboards and metal siding, placing them in random patterns that made no sense to my tired eyes. But one thing above all else was certain— we'd found our mysterious shop. The structures and leaning buttresses around the small business were completely covered in archaic diagrams.

Pulling up to the curb in front of the store, I parked and then turned off the engine. Tunuhun was staring at our surroundings, a wary look in his dark, thoughtful eyes. I could tell that he too was sensing that something wasn't quite right here. Turning to me, he pointed at the collection of unusual signage that was liberally festooned with feathers, bones, and other gewgaws.

"Kinnaŋaaq nappaŋagaa," he stated.

He was right; a madman had indeed built these. And it would be best for us to be on our guard from this point forward. But before I could comment on his astute observation, a slot in the heavily reinforced front door of the building shot open and the barrel of a rifle was slid out and aimed unerringly in our direction.

"Awright!" a crusty voice called from within the darkened interior. "That's far enough right there! Y'all better get yer hands where I can see 'em before I start shooting up that fancy ride of yours. I'm onta all yer tricks, you sneaky little bastards, and there ain't nothin more that you can do to stop me from leaving this blasted shithole of a town! I have had enough, and I aim to take the damn book with me when I goes!"

2

From the tone of the man's voice coming from behind that fortified door, I could tell that he was deadly serious. Glancing over at Tunuhun, I motioned for him to roll down the window.

"We're from Alaska," I shouted. "My Uncle Edward was an associate of yours."

"Ha!" the man retorted. "Edward is dead! Y'all can't trick me with that bunch a bullshit, you villainous swine!"

The shotgun blast was like a thunderclap, the back passenger side window exploding as the buckshot shattered the glass, sending shards of silvery particles ricocheting around the inside of the cockpit. Ducking down, I opened the door, and we both piled out on the driver's side, using the parked car as cover from the unexpected attack.

"Wait!" I called out. "We're not trying to trick you! I don't know who you think we are, but Edward *was* my uncle. We were sent here to see you by my aunt, Ataninnuaq. Please, we need your help!"

"Then prove to me you are who you say you are!" the man roared. "Tell me something that only Edward woulda knowd about me!"

I had to think fast before the situation got even more out of hand. I'd only been studying my uncle's tablet for a couple days now, but there had to be something in there that we could use to convince him. I pulled it from the case at my belt, turning it on, and then scrolling through the entries. "It says here in his personal journal that he entrusted you with a certain book about thirty-three years ago." I shouted from behind the car. "The book was a compilation of notes taken from a traveling monk who had access to a lot of other forbidden texts during the Inquisition. It was called, *Charmides Treatise on Mystical Maleficence.*"

"Anyone coulda knowd that!" he cried. "You ain't never gettin that book, and you ain't gettin me neither! I've had it, do you hear me! Iffen you got the stones, then bring it on! I'll be sendin you back to Hell soon enough!"

The shotgun went off again, the buckshot peppering the passenger side of the car. As the vehicle rocked with the impact, I cringed, hunkering lower behind the left front quarter panel. There had to be some way to appease this lunatic, a way to convince him that we weren't in league with whomever he was fighting against. In desperation, I scrolled through the information contained in the tablet, searching for something, anything, that would make him believe us. "Wait," I cried out, coming across a series of notations, "it says here you once got drunk with my uncle and lost a bet. You were supposed to recite from memory a passage from the *Necronomicon*, but you garbled the consonants. When you lost, he made you get a tattoo of something that he describes as an 'elder sign' on your left butt-cheek."

My announcement was met by dead silence from within the rundown building, but a moment later I heard a series of deadbolts being unlatched. Risking a look above the hood of the car, I was just in time to see the door creak open. The barrel of the gun poked out first and then beyond it, I saw a portly old man with shockingly white hair and a flabby, double chin. "Nobody coulda knowd that cept'in someone who knowd your uncle an me real well." His beady eyes darted about as he swung the rifle to and fro, making sure that the rest of his barricade-crowded lot was clear. "Y'all got two minutes to explain yourselves afore I open fire again."

I stood, holding my arms out in what I hoped would be a non-threatening manner. "My name's Gillam, and my companion and I were sent here by my aunt to ask for your help. Something's happened up near our village in the Brooks Range, something having to do with creatures that we've never seen nor heard of before. We were trapped for a time in their mountain base, and found a partial map incised upon a piece of stone tablet. What we saw in that artificial hive is a threat to the entire planet. We have to discover a way to stop these beings before it's too late, and we need your help to do it. My aunt says you know a lot about ancient languages and that you can possibly decipher this map fragment, perhaps even point us in the right direction so we can find the locations it refers to. Please, you're our only hope right now in figuring this out. My uncle once trusted you, came to you, and had you assist him with protecting things that he'd dug up during his explorations. All we ask now is that you honor his memory by working with us to prevent the possible annihilation of our entire species."

While I'd been speaking, the barrel of the man's rifle had lowered incrementally, until it pointed toward the ground instead of at us. After a moment of looking me over with an almost fanatical gleam in his squinty little eyes, he seemed to come to some kind of internal decision. Taking a last glance around to make sure the coast was clear, he waved us forward. "Awright, you've got my attention. Now hurry up and get yourselves in here afore somethin bad happens. As you may have noticed, it just ain't safe round these parts no more."

I felt I would have to agree with him there; this area had an unwholesomeness to it, a dark feeling that seeped into your bones and left an acrid taste at the back of your throat. Motioning to Tunuhun,

I moved around the car, taking the man's advice to get off the street as quickly as possible. I didn't know what was going on in this unnamed town, but I was certain of one thing—whatever was happening here, it was beyond our current understanding. As the man backed away, swinging the door open wider, Tunuhun and I hurried across the weed-choked sidewalk and then up the short flight of stairs to enter the building.

Once we'd moved into the shop's interior, the man slammed the door shut tight behind us and then locked the several large deadbolts located above the doorknob. After that he also took a hefty sized board and fitted it into brackets located to either side of the doorframe itself, further securing the entry with this additional, almost medieval precaution. The lighting was dim, but as my eyes adjusted to the wane illumination, I took a moment to scan our surroundings.

We were standing in a small room with many shelving units spaced at intervals across the center of the main floor. These cluttered displays were packed with oddities that I'd never before seen—trinkets and baubles, vessels filled with mysterious fluids, devices of unknown function, and even a large jar containing what appeared to be a pickled cat. Hanging from the rafters above us there were also bundles of dried herbs and pendants covered in hieroglyphic inscriptions. The walls looked as if they'd once contained racks filled with goods as well, but those had apparently all been torn down to make room for elaborate symbols painted in a dark reddish stain reminiscent of dried blood.

Just to the left was a long glass case filled with an assortment of other occult paraphernalia, which doubled as a front counter from the looks of it. And behind this case, just in front of an open archway at the back covered by a curtain of stringed beads, was a pedestal. It drew my curious attention because there was a soft glow emanating from it, almost as if there were some kind of energy field surrounding it on all sides. A book, which was opened at the center, was resting atop this shimmering podium. The lunatic saw me studying it and then stepped in front of us, barring our way forward.

He was overweight with wobbly double chins, yet his stubbled cheeks were sunken from some unknown hardship. Standing there, dressed in khaki pants and a gray woolen sweater, he seemed for a moment to become larger than life. Age-old eyes peered out at us from his wrinkle-furrowed features while the fringe of his starkly white hair floated in a curly halo around the bald dome of his head. The strange tableau held for a few seconds more before he glanced down, breaking the spell. Eyeballing the tablet gripped in my right hand, he grunted. "So, y'all weren't lying about your uncle's journal," he stated. "Well then, come on in already. We best be getting away from this here door—it ain't safe. Now, I'm a leavin here in the next few minutes, so please explain yourselves whilst I finish packin. I plan to be far away from this godforsaken place well afore sundown."

With that, he turned and went back around the counter, bending down to lift a heavy satchel from the floor and then setting it down next to the cash register. Into this already bulging valise, he began to stuff an assortment of objects—books, scrolls, and other bizarre items, all of them arcane in nature. Tunuhun set his hand on my arm, pointing to where there was a diagram inscribed on the opposite wall. It was very similar to the pictographs that we'd seen within the alien base up in the Brooks Range. Acknowledging his astute observation with a curt nod of my head, I turned my attention back to the old man, watching as he continued to pack.

"I hardly know where to begin," I said. Then, haltingly at first, but growing stronger in confidence as I went along, I told the tale. The only thing I left out was my mental link with that barrel-shaped being we'd released from imprisonment. I just felt it was something that I didn't want anyone else knowing right now, let alone a stranger. When I was through speaking, he stopped his methodical packing long enough to turn and study us, his stoic expression showing none of the surprise that I was expecting to see. Instead, he simply exhibited a hopeless weariness that made him look even older in the florescent overhead lighting.

"Well, it's looking like you boys is fucked," he finally said. "All of us are now. Them beings, them interstellar demons from another world? Well, they'll probably be takin over the planet soon, and there ain't a damn thing we can do about it." Shaking his head, he slapped the counter with an open palm. "I knowd somethin was a stirrin things up round here, I just knowd it! This town, as you may have noticed, has been through hell. Once, about thirty years ago, there was an event that happened round these parts. It very nearly opened a rift into our plane of existence an allowed somethin to come through, a being that shoulda never a been let outta whatever dimension it belongs in. Yet that one failed summoning started a whole buncha other troubles round here, and this 'ole town just was never the same after."

Waving a hand, he gestured broadly as he expanded upon the topic, pacing back and forth and growing more animated by the minute. "You see, this whole area sits atop a series of ley lines, streams of earth energy that intersect right here beneath our very feet. This source of mystical power draws a variety of unholy creatures from God knows where, causin them to gravitate to this here location. It somehow calls to them, I reckon, and to the legions of dark-hearted people who inevitably seek to gain control of its untapped potential. What you boys done went through up in them mountains was just another symptom of our ongoing descent into utter chaos. Them creatures you saw and the other ones they was a fightin? Well, they's all elder beings who once ruled this planet long afore we ever crawled outta the slime and evolved into the dominant species here on Earth. Them bug critters is called Mi-Go, and you better believe that they still exist here today, at least ones that weren't never caught up in this hibernation you speak of. They're a shifty bunch, always messin round with our government officials, stayin well behind the scenes and creating mischief wherever they go. Them other creatures? Well, they's called the Elder Things, and no one's seen nor heard from them in ages. Don't mean that they ain't still hangin round, though."

Coming back to our side of the counter, he laid a hand on my shoulder, giving it a hard squeeze. "There ain't nothin we can do about it, so here's my advice to you, friend—*run*. Get while the gettin's good! That's what I'm a doin, and I'd advise you two young bucks to do the same."

Shuffling off behind the counter again, he turned his back on us before continuing to pack. I glanced over at Tunuhun, but he just gazed at me, his complete confidence in my leadership evident from the look in his deep, dark eyes. This man, this eccentric, potentially insane old codger, had information we needed. His knowledge could perhaps be the key to finding out how to deal with the imminent invasion and also maybe tell us the best way to fight off the other dangers he'd so far only hinted at. I had to get him to become more forthcoming, attempt to earn his trust, or at the very least solicit his grudging assistance.

"You say there's been a history of unnatural events happening here," I said. "And you're clearly not surprised by what we experienced up in Alaska. So, what is it about our story that has any connection to what's been going on around here? Why, all of a sudden, after more than thirty years, are you prepared to run away? Why now? And if the threat is so much larger than all of us, and you're saying that it's entirely insurmountable, then why didn't you just leave here sooner? Why stay in this ill-omened place if you couldn't hope to triumph over the evil you believe will now consume us all?"

He stopped packing, his whole body shaking with barely contained emotion. When he turned to glance over his shoulder at us, there were tears spilling down the contours of his age-weathered cheeks. Wiping at the offending wetness with the angry swipe of a trembling hand, he took in a deep, shuddering breath. "You boys don't know what I've been through," he said in a quavering voice. "I am not. . . not what you would consider a brave man. But after what happened here so many years ago, I thought I could do some good, thought I could maybe fight off some of what was happenin round here. I had friends back then, people I knowd I could count on, people that mattered to me, that looked up to me for help and support. But I failed. I failed them all!"

Rubbing a hand over his distraught features, he took another deep breath, collecting himself before going on. "The townsfolk round here, well, they all succumbed to the darkness one by one," he said, "slipping away into them tunnels beneath this place, never to be seen nor heard from again. Things you don't even wanna know about is livin down there in the dark, things that just ain't right. On top of all that, there's a presence that's taken root here, and damned if I know what it is, but it's only grown stronger the longer I've stayed. For a time, I was able to hold my own—been fightin them demons with what little power I gained from all them things I done studied over the years. But it jus ain't enough no more. Fact is, it weren't *never* enough!"

He took a step toward me, frustration evident in every line of his quivering body. "Deep in them tunnels, somethin's coming to a head," he insisted. "There's somthin about to happen round here, somethin I can *feel* deep down in my bones! Your tale don't surprise me none 'cause it's just like what's been happenin all over the world right now. This whole planet is going to Hell-in-a-handbasket and there ain't no way to stop it. Them Mi-Go you woke up, them Elder Things you released? That's just like adding fuel to an already roaring fire. Soon this world will no longer be under our control, iffen it ever truly was. The best thing I can do now is to take this collection of occult knowledge, these tomes filled with powerful spells and incantations, and disappear, get them away from whatever's about to happen round here and hide them from all who'd seek to use them against us. It's the only way to prevent that now, don't you see?"

The man wasn't making a lot of sense, but I could tell he believed every word of what he was saying. And who was I to doubt him? Who was I to disbelieve the things he was telling us after all we'd been through in that godforsaken hive? If what he was saying were true, then the threat to the planet was even greater than I'd realized. Yet there had to be a way to stop this evil from spreading, some way that we could deal with what was going on around us right now while simultaneously attempting to overcome what was happening on a global level.

I found myself clenching the stone fragment in my pocket, the piece of map tile that Tunuhun had taken from the cavern we'd fallen into during our battle with the Mi-Go. If there were some way to translate its cryptic inscriptions, could it take us to another place that held more of their advanced technology? Might we then be able to use this technology, to figure out some way to turn it against whatever was menacing our planet, even if what we found was beyond our current understanding? It didn't matter that we might not be able to utilize it right away; we had to start somewhere—begin to arm ourselves against these existential threats. To give up now would be to just roll over and accept our fate, and I, for one, was not prepared to do that just yet. For now, I would fight back with every resource we could lay our hands on.

"Please," I said, taking out the chunk of inscribed rock, "if there's any chance we can stop them, we have to attempt it. You mentioned that you once believed there was a way to prevent them from doing what they're doing, and it was because of this belief that you've stayed here for so many years battling against them. To give up now would make the deaths of all the people you once cared about meaningless. Will you throw away their sacrifice? What if they were here right now? What would they say to you? What would they ask you to do?" I gestured with the fractured mosaic I held in my outstretched hand. "With this map fragment, we could locate other bases that these entities may not know about yet. That hive we found up in Alaska had been buried under tons of ice for many years. When these things awoke, they didn't even know what a human being was, let alone that others of their kind were still present in the here and now. Those Elder Things seemed to know even less. We can use that to our advantage."

"These beings possess technology greater than anything we presently have, and they don't even know that we've figured out a way to locate more of their ancient installations," I continued. "Their forces are scattered, beaten back by the government agents I told you of. Even if they did manage to get a message out to their home world, their brethren here on Earth still won't know what's going on yet. These are creatures that have been hibernating for hundreds of thousands of years. The technology they had back then, even their style of communication, may be too archaic for their contemporary counterparts to understand. If we can figure out where this map leads to, we could stay one step ahead of them. To run and hide, to not even give it our best shot? Well, that would be an act more shameful than the cowardice that you've so readily admitted to. Besides, what better place to hide the books you're guarding than in the Mi-Go's own long-forgotten strongholds?"

The man glared at me for a moment but then held out his hand. Without hesitation, I handed him the chunk of stone. "Hmmmm. . ." he muttered to himself as he studied it. "This is quite interestin. I can read some of it, and it indicates a geometric pattern of sorts. And there's a smidgen of their language written here along the edges. Perhaps I can puzzle the rest of this out, given time. Or perhaps I might just fail again, like I did afore. But I reckon you're right just the same; we do have to at least try. And they sure won't know what we're up to iffen we stay off of their radar. We can hide them old books while we're at it, maybe even get a few steps out in front of what's a comin. You!" Pointing at Tunuhun, he indicated the ancient volume resting on the pedestal. "Bring me that tome, and mind that you don't wrinkle them pages! Iffen I can get a better translation of these pictographs, then maybe we could get started on figurin out the coordinates to the next one of them hidden forts of theirs."

Tunuhun narrowed his eyes at the man's commanding tone, but then shrugged it off as he walked behind the counter and lifted the heavy book gently from its resting place. As he turned back with the item clutched firmly in his large, capable hands, there was a rupturing noise, like river ice cracking after a spring thaw. Before we could react, the floor under the podium exploded, sending shards of wood spraying out across the room. Within the depths of this newly formed hole, I saw a plethora of hideous, canid beings reaching up with dozens of taloned hands. In a matter of seconds, they'd latched on to my friend, grasping, clawing, and pulling him inexorably into the rent in the floor below him. Accompanied by a guttural barking chorus, like the collective yapping of a pack of slavering hyenas, he was dragged down into the abyss, taking the book with him as he disappeared beneath the shattered floorboards.

3

After a moment of shocked incredulity, my mind still reeling from the suddenness of the attack, I lunged forward, dropping to my knees next to the jagged rent in the floor. Gazing into its depths, I could see nothing but inky blackness. As the overhead light fixture swung back and forth with a rusty creaking noise, I cried out into that well of stygian gloom, "*Tunuhun!*"

Yet there was no response. Just the hollow echoes of my voice rebounding off of the walls of the room around me.

While I sat in horrified indecision, the old man scrambled over to the lip of the hole. With an exclamation that sounded much like a snarl, his wild eyes scanned the darkness below us. "That shouldna happened," he said. "There's at least two feet of concrete in this building's foundation alone, and I've spent a great deal of time warding this area on top of that. I may not be the bravest person round these parts, but my wards is strong! They done held for the last thirty years, and I strengthen them almost ever day! There ain't nothin that I knows of round here that coulda broke them, let alone dug through all that concrete." Grabbing my shoulder, his jowls shook as spittle flew from his lips. "The book!" he cried in delayed reaction, eyes glimmering with maddened intensity. "We gotta get that damn thing back afore they can put it to use down there!" With that, he sat at the edge of the gaping wound in the floor and then swung his legs into the abyss, grasping the splintered edges of the ruptured floorboards in preparation of lowering himself into the unfathomable void below us. Before he could throw his life away in what I considered to be a futile effort, I reached out to steady him on the verge of his plunge, stopping him just short of disaster.

"Wait," I said. "Let's gather up some supplies along with our wits before we do anything rash. We'll need to be able to safely traverse this hole and then track those things, destroy them if necessary, in order to save my friend and get the book back. Tell me," I asked, swallowing the rising panic that was threatening to overwhelm me, "how do we even know that he's still alive?"

The old man reached over to grab my arm with a surprising amount of strength. "You don't understand! There's a good chance your friend is still alive, but iffen we don't get that book back, we're fucked! With that there book, them things can open up a portal into our world, a way to let the being they worship appear in the flesh! Iffen that happens. . .

well, that'll be the end right there, the end of you, me, your friend—the end of everythin!"

I gazed at him, this portly shell of a man. He must have been well over sixty years old, yet here he was, trapped in the grip of lunacy, proposing that we venture into the unknown without even a flashlight to guide us. Even though my mind was screaming at me to do the same, I knew it was a fool's errand. There was gear we needed to collect—weapons, rope, medical supplies—that could help us to succeed. And though he claimed that Tunuhun was still alive, I didn't even know what we were up against. I needed more information, but also realized that time was of the essence. Gathering myself, I rose to my feet, pulling the distraught proprietor up with me. "I have items in the trunk of the car, equipment that can help us. You need to calm yourself enough to think rationally, to tell me what we'll be facing down there. In the meantime, start grabbing anything that may be of help in defeating those monsters. We're going to have to act fast, but also be ready to defend ourselves. Don't you agree?"

"Y-yes. . ." he stammered, "you're right of course. We do need to be better prepared." Twisting out of my grip, he turned away, pulling a rucksack from beneath the counter and then stacking items from the display case next to it. After he had a fair amount of paraphernalia built up, he added the shotgun to the pile and then began stuffing his pockets full of spare ammo. "Them things," he said. "I don't know exactly what they were, but I suspect I knows what they *used* to be. This here town has been infested with them sorta critters for ages, probably hundreds of years. But they shouldna never been able to breach my wards, let alone dig through several feet of gravel and concrete to reach the floor beneath us. Them spells I cast is more than enough to hold off your average pack of ghouls, and they sure as hell ain't never been strong enough to dig through a building's foundation afore. Now, hard-packed dirt, clay, roots? You betcha. Them claws is deadly sharp, and they're like a damn pack of burrowing weasels when it comes right down to it. But concrete? No, this here be a whole new type a critter that I ain't never seen afore, somethin different than what's been livin round here all these years."

He paused, mopping sweat from his brow with an old rag, the sparse curls of his white hair standing out in a disheveled halo around his bald head. "As for your friend, well I done already told you how the townsfolk round here were drawn into them tunnels, right? I suspect with most of them dead now, it's more than likely them critters is gonna need your friend for some kinda ritual, probably the one that opens up a gateway into our world. They're for sure gonna need a live sacrifice to make that happen, and there ain't no two ways about it. So's we gots to get to him afore they start that ritual, and we gots to get that damn book back no matter what else happens!"

37

This whole situation was insane. Yet, after what we'd gone through in Alaska, I'd known this quest of ours wasn't going to be easy. In fact, the things I'd experienced combined with the visions I'd suffered from the creature who still rode my subconscious thoughts had convinced me that our task was going to be monumentally difficult. But I had hoped we'd be able to unscramble more of the puzzle without being embroiled so quickly in yet another perilous confrontation. Squaring my shoulders, I stiffened my slipping resolve. I had to do this, not only for myself and the life of my friend, but also for the survival of the entire human race. As I considered my options, thoughts of my own cultural upbringing and my aunt's indomitable spirit surged to the forefront of my mind, inspiring me to solidify my wavering conviction into unbreakable purpose. "I am called Gillam, and my friend's name is Tunuhun," I intoned. "We are of the Inuit peoples. And whatever else happens, I will not let him die down there alone in the dark."

The man gazed at me with compassion in his fever-bright eyes. "Well," he said softly, "that might be beyond our ability to stop at this point, but we'll do what we can, that we will." Clearing his throat, he offered me his hand. "The name's Jarrod, and I guess you already done figured out that I used to run this here shop, well, back in the day that is. Like I said afore, I've been fightin against them demons for nigh on forty years now. But a few days back, things just went plum crazy round here. Them critters began testin my wards ever night, an packs of ghouls was a comin round the lot outside causin all kinds of a ruckus. Been getting the feelin somethin was goin on down below as well, somethin big. You know, I always figured I was doin somethin good, somethin noble, by protectin them books, but in these last few days I done realized that I were just foolin myself. There ain't no way I coulda held back whats a comin, not here, not now. That's why I decided to take them books and get the hell outta town."

Grasping the man's proffered hand, I shook it firmly. "Together, you and I will beat this thing," I told him. "I don't know what all you've been through, don't even know what we're really up against, yet together we are stronger than they can ever know. Saving Tunuhun's life is my top priority, but I don't see any reason we can't focus on both tasks simultaneously. I have skills that could be useful, tools and weapons out in the trunk of the car that may come in handy. Surely, between the two of us, we can hold these creatures back long enough to rescue both my companion and that book you've been protecting. So, let's just focus all of our energy on that for right now. Once we've completed that task, then we can get back to worrying about the rest of the world."

His eyes bore into mine, an intense, searching gaze that seemed to pin me to the spot. But then the curious sensation ended as he released my hand and turned back to his rucksack. "Awright," he said, continuing to stuff things into the sack, "you go on and get them things you need from the car. I gots a few surprises left for what dwells down there in the darkness, some things they ain't gonna like, to be sure."

Chortling to himself, he continued to sort through what he'd already taken from the display case, while I made my way around the counter and then headed for the door. I didn't know exactly what we'd be facing in those tunnels. Ghouls and other otherworldly threats were mostly unknown to me except for the creatures I'd encountered in that mountainous hive a few days ago. But there was one thing that I did know for sure—if they were made of flesh and blood, then we could kill them. With that in mind, I unbarred the door and then carefully exited the shop, jogging down the walkway to the parked car while keeping an eye on my surroundings at all times. Grabbing the keys from my pocket, I popped the trunk and found the supplies inside that Tunuhun and I had gathered from my uncle's safe house.

There were coils of rope, flashlights, flares, a variety of medical supplies, and weapons of various sizes and calibers. For this excursion, I chose a Mossberg 500 tactical shotgun and a Glock 19 handgun with plenty of spare ammo. There was no telling what we'd find, and I wanted to be ready for anything. I was already dressed in warm clothing since it was getting on toward the end of August, but I grabbed an extra jacket, just in case. Gathering up a selection of the other items, I used a small backpack to store most of it and then made sure the pistol was holstered securely under my left arm before closing the trunk.

I took one last glance around just for safety's sake, but the twilight-lit neighborhood seemed quiet, almost unnaturally so. Whatever those things were, they seemed to have gotten what they were after for the time being. There was nothing else going on in these empty streets right now except small whorls of dust and leaves being driven by the wind. With a shrug, I shouldered the shotgun and then headed back inside.

As I entered the building, locking the stout door behind me, I found the man standing by the hole with the rucksack strapped across his broad back. He seemed to be studying something as I approached, shining a flashlight down into the depths of the void before him. Peering over his shoulder, I caught a glimpse of the interior of the pit. The sides of it were unnaturally smooth, and I wondered what could have done that without making a great deal of noise. It was uncanny. Jarrod turned to me with a bemused expression painted across his florid face.

"It looks like they done learned themselves some new tricks," he said. "This here hole is as cleanly cut as I ever did see, and I don't have the foggiest idea on hows they did it without me knowing." Shining the light around the edges of the shaft just beneath the splintered flooring, he bent down to study it further. "It's like they done moved the concrete and soil all at once, simply extracted it somehow. Get a gander at how regular them walls are. This ain't somethin they done natural like. I woulda heard them had they been diggin round down there all this time. And them wards they broke through just below the pedestal itself was incredibly strong. I spent a lot of time perfectin them rituals, and there ain't nothin I knows of what coulda breached them like they did. No, these here critters, whatever they may be now, well, they musta had some kinda help."

"You told us there was an event that happened here many years ago," I said. "But you haven't elaborated on it. If we're going to go down into those tunnels together, I'd like to know more about it. What happened here so many years ago to make this a town inhabited only by the lost souls of those no longer truly alive?"

His eyes were shadowed, taking on a vacant look as he gazed into some far distant past. After a few moments of silent introspection, he heaved a great sigh and then refocused on me once more. "Well, like I said afore, this is a place of great power, a nexus if you will, with them lines of force intersecting below us. And places like that, well, they draws a certain type of people, mostly them that's into the dark arts. What happened here over thirty years ago is a long story best told at another time perhaps. The important thing for you to know right now is that there's a deity them cultists and ghouls all worship round here. They attempted to perform a ritual to summon that foul creature into our world, but it didn't go quite as they planned."

His words once would have made me scoff. Cultists, rituals, deities from beyond time and space? Not so long ago it would have all sounded ridiculous to me. Yet now, after what I'd seen in the depths of the alien base we'd found up in the Brooks Range, what I'd witnessed staring back at me from within the hellish globe in their central hibernation chamber, I could certainly believe that there were many things out there that we have very little understanding of. The creatures I'd fought in those mountains were from the stars, an unfamiliar species with a much higher level of technology than our own. Was this any different? Perhaps this deity he spoke of was just another entity that existed outside of our limited realm of understanding, a being so far advanced from us that it seemed to be almost magical in nature. The creatures beneath our feet, they could be anything. But what if they were just another race that originated from somewhere beyond our own galaxy, what if the being they all worshiped was just one more extraterrestrial lifeform bent on the destruction of all mankind? Could that not seem, to those of a lesser intelligence, like these creatures were godlike themselves?

"We will leave the rest of that tale for later," I agreed, coming back from my inopportune musings, "yet that still doesn't tell me much about those things that took my friend. You called them 'ghouls.' Surely you can't mean the ghouls from out of old fairy tales and legends?"

"Well, yes and no, so to speak," he said. "These things are humanoid in semblance yet very different from you an me. Like in them tales, they're usually wont to hang out beneath graveyards, feeding on the flesh of the dead, breeding, keeping pretty much to themselves. But the ones round here are also mighty smart and much bolder than the ones you done read about in them nursery rhymes. You can expect to be attacked on sight. They have claws that will rip a man to shreds in two shakes of a coon's tail, and teeth like those of a timber wolf. On top of that, there are even more dangerous things hidden in them tunnels, things I ain't never seen, but have heard of. Some friends of mine, those that lived to tell the tale, well, they said there's more than a few nasty critters down there that you and I don't ever want nothin to do with. That's why we'll be taken along these 'lil' babies."

Digging into the pocket of the heavy, brown leather jacket he'd donned, he pulled out a couple of necklaces. They were strung from thick, braided cords and had a series of beads interspaced between pieces of bone on either side of a central medallion. The medallion itself was also made from some type of bone, roughly circular in shape, with small glyphs inscribed all around the circumference. At the center of each one was a smear of what appeared to be dried blood.

"These," he said, holding one out to me, "were made from the bones I took from ghouls that used to dwell in them tunnels. I spent a great deal of time and effort on them, hoping I could use them iffen I ever got brave enough to take the fight to them instead of staying up here in this damn store of mine. I even made extras. I guess I always hoped I would eventually have help with all of this. Now seems like a good time to try them out, although I ain't promisin you nothin. If I made them correct, well, then they should provide some protection against them things, drive them away or at least hide us from their senses for a time as we try an sneak by 'em. Iffen they don't work, well then I suppose we'll have one hell of a fight on our hands."

He put his on while I was still studying my own. After a moment, I placed the foul thing around my neck. At this point, I'd take whatever help I could get, whether or not I believed in it. Then, moving closer to the hole, I got down on my knees and used my own flashlight to investigate. The walls of the shaft were smooth and regular, almost perfectly circular in size and definition. I could see layers of concrete, then gravel, and then hard-packed earth, but they'd all been sheared off and somehow fused into a glossy, smooth surface as far down as I could see. The beam of light wasn't powerful enough to reach the bottom, so I had no idea how deep it was. Sitting back on my heels, I pulled a flare from my backpack and struck the cap, lighting it with a twist of my hands. Then, as the torch blazed up into hissing red flames, I tossed it into the pit before us.

It was a long time before it reached the bottom.

Down there, deep in the murky darkness, I could just make out the small circle of light from the sputtering torch. There were no other details I could ascertain from where I was kneeling. *Where was Tunuhun, and what were they doing to him?* I wondered. Would he even be still alive when we found him? Was it possible to rescue him from those things and still get out of there in one piece? I guessed we were about to find out.

Uncoiling the rope from my pack, I tied one end of it around the heavy, built-in shelving units behind us, and then cast its remaining length down into the hole.

4

Now that I was staring down into the abyss before me, the reality of the situation started to sink in. Reaching out, I placed my hand on the counter to steady myself as I was momentarily overcome by a surge of indecision. These things, they'd taken Tunuhun, dragged him down into this hole in the floor right before my eyes. And I currently had little idea of what they were or even how to fight them. Once again, I found myself in an untenable position. Even though I was raised as a hunter in a small village, I'd also attended college outside of the state of Alaska, furthering my education over the course of several years. This experience had opened my eyes to how the world outside of my small community functioned. Yet to be faced with such a catastrophic event in the here and now, I was a soul divided. One part of me was calculating how best to hunt these creatures, trusting in the skills I'd learned while growing up to guide and protect me through this dangerous mission. But the other half of me was thinking how unrealistic this scenario was to begin with, what the odds were that I could even succeed, and how it would impact the rest of the world should we fail. On top of that, my emotions, at first suppressed by the shock of this unexpected event and then bolstered by thoughts of my strong cultural heritage, were now boiling over with grief and mounting anxiety. I could not bear to lose another friend like I'd done with Opeim; that was still a raw, open wound in my heart that had not yet even begun to heal. Rubbing a trembling hand across my suddenly chilled features, I steeled myself to once more venture into the darkened unknown, to face soulless creatures that I had no true understanding of, with no inkling of their skills, intents, or range of abilities.

"Are you awright?" Jarrod asked, placing a hand on my shoulder. "You look like you done seen a ghost or somethin."

Somehow managing to overcome my internal distress, I shook off the feelings of mounting dread and cleared my throat. "I'm okay," I assured him. "I just hadn't expected to be doing something quite this dangerous so soon after what happened up in the Brooks Range. I suppose from now on I'll just have to be ready for anything. How did you hold out here by yourself for so many years? How did you manage to fight on and on with these things right beneath your feet and still retain your sanity?"

His smile was a little deranged as his flint-like eyes glinted in the fluorescent lighting. "Some might say that I didn't," he said with a chuckle. "Stay sane, that is. Sure, I been fightin them things a long time now. Got me some stories that would most likely curl the hair on your head just to hear them. But it definitely takes somethin out of you, demands somethin from you in ways that tend to twist you up inside. I don't think I made it this far with all my marbles still in the same bag, iffen you catch my drift. But one thing's for damn sure—they didn't send me packin, an they ain't never got ahold of that there book. At least til now." Slapping me on the shoulder, he hefted his shogun and placed it in the crook of his arm. "But don't you worry none; me and 'ole Bessie here have got your back one hunnerd percent."

Somehow that didn't make me feel any more confident of our success.

Struggling to pull myself together, I hefted my pack, settling it onto my back and then checking my weapons to make sure they were loaded and ready. If nothing else, we were going to make one hell of a ruckus down there if those things attacked. But between the spells this old man knew and the tracking skills I possessed, I figured we at least had a fighting chance of finding Tunuhun and the book before they got too far ahead of us. Squaring my shoulders, I decided that the longer we waited, the farther away those things were going to get. With that in mind, I tested the rope to make sure it was secure. Then, turning around, I knelt and eased myself over the edge of the hole, being careful not to impale myself on the sharp edges of the broken floorboards.

The climb down was arduous, but I soon reached the bottom and then steadied the rope as the much heavier man clambered down, almost falling the last few feet and very nearly crushing me beneath his plummeting bulk. But he managed to right himself, swinging around a few times before scrambling the rest of the way to the ground. He was panting heavily as he landed beside me, leaning over to place his hands on his knees for a moment while sucking in huge lungfuls of air.

While he caught his breath, I took the opportunity to look around. We were in a rough-shaped tunnel hewn from hard-packed dirt and rock. Of the perfect circle of concrete and gravel that had made up the foundation of the dwelling above us, there was no sign. It was as if something had carved a circular core sample from the area right below where the book had been stored and then made the detritus vanish into thin air. There wasn't even any leftover debris except shattered pieces of the broken pedestal and some splintered floorboard remnants. Using my flashlight, I studied the tunnel walls and found them to be regular and smooth as well, without claw markings or other signs of digging tools that I'd expected to find.

"This is beyond what them things shoulda been able to do," Jarrod said, eyeing the tunnel surrounding us. "They had help, and of the magical sort iffen I don't miss my guess. We could be in a helluva lot more trouble down here than I originally figured. Whelp!" he said, hitching up his britches, "There ain't nothin else for it—let's go get them sons-o-bitches!"

Taking the shotgun from his back, where he'd slung it while descending the rope, he reached under the barrel and switched on the attached light, sending a strong beam out ahead of us to pierce the eerily quiet darkness.

While I approved of his enthusiasm, I had to place my hand on his shoulder to restrain him. There was no sense in going off half-cocked. When hunting an animal, it was always best to stalk it intelligently and with a true sense of purpose. He looked at me, his eyes wild in the thin light coming down from above, and I thought for a moment that he was going to strike me. Then, he just smiled, an unsavory grin that sent small chills racing up and down my spine. Shrugging off the uncomfortable sensation, I motioned for him to wait while I further assessed the situation.

Crouching down, I studied the ground in front of us. The tunnel sloped gently away, with several sets of footprints visible in the dirt-strewn path. There was no way for me to be certain of how many of them there were; the tracks were far too muddled. But I estimated at least twenty or more had been in the party that abducted Tunuhun. It made me wonder just how they'd managed to climb the near-vertical shaft to get to the floor above us. Running the light up the walls to either side provided no further information; how they'd accomplished this feat of inhuman dexterity remained a mystery. Listening intently for a few moments, I thought I heard some screeching followed by a thin, human-sounding wail coming from not too far ahead. Rising from my crouch, I motioned Jarrod to follow as I took off after the creatures, hoping against hope that Tunuhun would still be alive when we caught up to them.

The tunnel descended for quite a while before leveling off and coming to an area which held a variety of other openings splitting off from the main corridor. Yet I could easily discern from the markings along the floor which direction they were heading. There were other prints leading off in all directions to be sure, but the ones that we followed were the freshest by far. Without worrying overmuch about what was lurking in those other side tunnels, or even pausing to study the multitudes of branching pathways, I increased our pace, hoping to catch up to the creatures before they got too far ahead. Jarrod kept up with me as we hurried along, shining the flashlight before us, and ignoring the pungent stench that rose like a sullen mist as we probed deeper into this realm of stygian gloom.

Before long, we came to the end of the tunnel and stepped out onto a ledge that overlooked a small cavern. Below us there was an abundance of fluorescent fungi, including many gigantic mushroom species that I had never before seen. The ceiling had a plethora of stalactites as well, while across from us resided a huge stone archway which appeared to have been blown apart at some point in the far distant past. Chunks of moss-covered debris rested in front of this foreboding aperture, and a vast row of arcane sigils were carved along the edges of its pitted circumference. These markings glowed with a light of their own, making me feel even more uneasy, like I stood facing something beyond the paltry knowledge of all humanity, a vast emptiness which swirled with an inner consciousness I could not immediately fathom. Fortunately, the pack of creatures that we'd been following had passed by this eerily-lit entrance to instead make for another exit farther down the way. The passage they were now heading for was much different than the ancient archway, more of mortared stone and human construction techniques than the shattered portal's more ambiguous nature. But it was the beasts themselves, now that we'd caught up to them, that drew my unwavering attention.

They were humanoid in shape from what I could see in the green glow of the fungi, yet there was something distinctly wrong about them. They were thin, disjointed things, creatures out of a terrible nightmare, with huge, luminescent eyes and mouths full of what could only be described as row upon row of sharp canine teeth. Of lips and eyelids, I saw no sign. These hideous monstrosities loped along in a tight grouping, holding on to my friend from all sides as they carried him in the midst of their angular flight. This made it difficult for me to determine what their bodies actually looked like since they were packed together so closely. For a brief moment, Tunuhun saw me from where he was being jostled along, his own eyes like twin points of normalcy within that terrible collection of ocular-orbed abominations. And in that split second of contact, the barrel-shaped being that rode my thoughts, who'd been absent from my mind for so long now that I'd nearly forgotten it, surged across the link, filling my head full of vivid visuals, things that I could scarcely process or even try to understand.

The images were dim and blurry, hard to comprehend, and much different than what it had shared with me in the past. From them, I somehow got the impression that the creature was now deep beneath the sea, swimming along the bottom in a lightless void which swirled with other denizens of that unseen world. There was the sensation of great pressure as well, the weight of thousands of gallons of seawater bearing down on me, and I stumbled from the impact of it all, struggling as I sought to untangle myself from this being's unwanted perceptions. It was trying to tell me something, something of importance to my own quest here beneath this unnamed town, yet whatever that message was, I could not get past the initial feelings of compression long enough to understand it. A sharp sting across my face brought me back to myself, to find Jarrod holding me up by the front of my jacket. Belatedly, I reached out to ward off another open-handed blow.

"Sorry I had to slap you there, friend," he whispered. "But they's a gettin away and this is no time for you to go all funny on me!"

I tore myself from his grasp, turning my attention back to the scene unfolding below us in the fungus-filled chamber. The creatures were now almost to the other doorway leading out of the cavern, Tunuhun still held firmly within their multitudinous grip. He was watching me, I could tell. Even though I could no longer see his face among the crowd I could still sense that it was so. There was movement out of the corner of my eye, and I struck Jarrod's gun barrel down before he could fire the weapon.

"Wait!" I said. "Isn't there something else you can do, something that will slow them down without risking Tunuhun's life?"

"His life is already *at* risk!" he replied. "We gots to stop them from leaving this here cave afore they can get into them other passageways. We could risk losing the book if we don't act now! And I can't do nothin from here with what little power I have, at least not afore they gets through that other door they's a headin toward!"

There was no way to outflank them, no time to get into a position where we would effectively block their path. We could continue to stalk them, but Jarrod was right—we'd easily lose them if the tunnels below were cut from solid rock. There would be no tracks for us to follow, and we had little idea of what awaited us beyond that second door. We had to do something now, something that would stop them from escaping. But before I could decide on a new course of action, a low, moaning cry rose up from the group.

They'd seen us.

As they came to a full stop, bathed in the eerie glow of the surrounding fungi, I could finally get a better look at the pack of ghastly abominations tangled together in a close circle around my friend. From what I could make out in the faint, greenish illumination, they were spindly and gaunt creatures with overlarge heads dominated by owl-like, lidless eyes. Tunuhun struggled at the center of this repellent mob as one of the beings suddenly stepped away from the tightly packed hodgepodge of angular limbs and oddly-shaped body parts. As it strode forward on its own, an ethereal nimbus sprang up around it, revealing more of its disturbing anatomy within this shimmering aura.

It was tall and gangly, its limbs sparsely muscled and whip-cord thin, with a stretching of mottled skin that was drawn tight across its frame like an ill-fitting suit of fleshy latex. At the knees and ankles, the joints were bent at odd angles, like those of a deer, and its hands were much larger than my own, with talons like a predatory bird. Yet its face, wreathed now in the pale, yellowish light emanating from its own body, was by far the worst part of its astounding physiology. Large, soulless eyes stared back at me from an elongated skull, the horrific, fang-filled jaws taking up a full three quarters of the remaining surface area. While I watched in terrified fascination, this oral cavity opened with a ghastly parting of those needle-like denticulations, and I saw a long, black tongue slither forth as it began to chant.

Jarrod leveled his weapon again, and this time I joined him. We had to take this creature out before it finished casting whatever hellish spell that it was preparing. With the hairs on the back of my neck standing straight up, I sighted down the barrel of my shotgun, preparing to attack even as the rest of the mob behind the grotesque warlock began to chant in unison. Yet before we could open fire, there was a great, rustling movement from above us as the stalactites began to shift and flutter, groaning as they shook themselves loose, dislodging a hail of small pebbles and other debris.

Backing away, I struggled to comprehend this new development, my shocked confusion making me briefly forget the loaded gun I still held in my trembling grasp. Regaining control of myself, I groped through my jacket pocket for the flashlight and then switched it on. Once I managed to shine it upward, I was completely taken aback by what I found there.

What I had mistaken as stalactites were now revealed to be a large number of folded wings, the points of which had been facing downward from the creatures who were perching above us. These beings were serpentine in nature, their long, sinuous black coils running around and between the outcroppings of rocky ceiling they'd been nesting upon. As their great, bat-like wings spread wide and they began to soar through the fetid air, I knew that our doom was sealed.

At that moment, there was a hissing shout from the chanting leader of the group holding Tunuhun. With that command, many of its brethren split from the pack of massed bodies to lope toward us at an alarming rate of speed, howling in long-, drawn-out ululations. Confronted by this two-pronged attack, we bolted, turning to run back into the tunnel we'd so recently vacated. But that corridor was now crawling with more of the canid creatures. They swarmed from every aperture and opening, tangling together as they came at us en masse, like one huge organism made from multiple limbs and biting, gnashing jaws. As this horrific conglomeration of howling death rolled toward us, boiling forth from the depths and surging down the surrounding tunnels in a hideous, almost solid glut of feral bodies, I turned to face the flying nightmares closing on us from behind.

They were sinuous in shape, their looping, blackened coils whipping through the air as they came at us, enormous wings flapping with stunning rapidity as they dove and soared around each other in intricate displays of swirling dexterity. I fired my weapon at the same time as Jarrod, our backs pressed hard against the wall next to the tunnel opening, yet our bullets had little effect.

In this nightmare realm, we were outnumbered and surrounded, our weapons useless against such overwhelming odds. Steeling myself, I continued to blast away at the oncoming horde, determined to sell my life as dearly as possible before succumbing to the final embrace of all-consuming death.

5

As the abhorrent creatures surged forward, yapping and howling like a pack of feral dogs, the swarm of huge, serpentine monstrosities swirled down on us from above. Our weapons were having very little effect, and it was sending me spiraling into panicked hysteria. Why had I decided we'd be able to come down into this pit of unknown evil and rescue Tunuhun with any degree of success? A shriek of all-consuming despair grew within me and then forced its way up through my esophagus. As I opened my mouth to vent a vibrant cry of deranged defiance, the loathsome creatures continued their onward rush, but for some unknown reason Jarrod suddenly ceased firing his weapon. As I continued to blast away at the oncoming hordes, I noticed he was now rifling through his jacket pockets with an air of maddened intensity.

A crazed grin spread across his florid features as he found what he was groping after, and he then hurled the object to the ground before us. There was a brilliant flash, and suddenly the creatures were screeching and clawing at each other as they fought to get away from the blinding illumination. In those few brief moments of respite, I squinted my tear-blurred vision against the dazzling light, searching desperately for any means of escape. There had to be some way to survive this, and I clung to that feeble hope as I sought to distance ourselves from the tangle of limbs, wings, and snapping jaws that now swirled like a beast-filled maelstrom beyond the intense glare of the device Jarrod had thrown.

And there it was; just to our left and down a short incline was an opening unlike the others we'd seen so far, and it was also strangely devoid of any adversaries. We hadn't noticed it before because it had been cloaked in shadows and hidden behind another outcropping of rock. This aperture was built into the surrounding stone of the cavern wall, but appeared to be meticulously decorated with intricate motifs of an unusual design. Wasting no more time in studying these bizarre markings, I grabbed Jarrod's arm and then shoved him toward the bolt hole. If nothing else, we could perhaps hold them off more successfully from that vantage point once we got inside. With no other viable options presenting themselves, we scrambled into the dubious safety of this mysterious tunnel as the flash of ultra-bright light slowly dwindled away behind us.

I didn't know what he'd thrown, yet its effect upon these creatures was not unusual for beings that dwelled forever in perpetual darkness. However, as the flare of brilliance faded, the denizens of this nocturnal netherworld regrouped and then came boiling back toward us. After checking to make sure there were no unpleasant surprises awaiting us within the tunnel's shadowy depths, I turned to face the oncoming onslaught, leveling my shotgun with as much bravado as I could muster. Yet outside of our newfound place of refuge there now reigned an almost utter lack of hostilities. Staring in bemusement at this total reversal of fortune, I saw that the spindly-legged canines were all slinking back toward their leader, once more highlighted only by the greenish glow of the fungus growing across the cavern floor. And aside from the rustle of wings and a few falling pebbles, there was no further sign of the winged serpents either. I could only assume they'd flown back up to roost on the ceiling above us.

Moving cautiously, I leaned out of the tunnel mouth and shone my flashlight out across the fungus-filled area, the adrenalized fear which had fueled me but moments before fading into puzzlement. Squinting my eyes, I was just able to make out the creatures rejoining their brethren and caught a brief glimpse of Tunuhun still being held within their midst, his face a mask of stoic resignation. But then the leader of these subhuman fiends came forward to stare at me with his huge, unblinking eyes. It seemed to me that he was grinning, yet with that many rows of teeth I could hardly be sure. After studying me for a few moments, he spread his arms wide and then bowed deeply, his mouth cracking open to utter a benevolent sounding string of incomprehensible phrases. The incongruity of it all had me greatly perplexed. Was I going mad, or had this thing just graced me with a solemn benediction?

As I stood pondering this bewildering occurrence, Jarrod put a hand on my shoulder. "We havfta find some other way round this here cave," he said. "Them hunting horrors nesting above it are too much for us to handle—we ain't got nothin that'll even scratch 'em since they ain't truly here to begin with."

I had no idea what he meant by the cryptic remark, but right now I had bigger concerns. "Why do you suppose they've stopped?" I said. "And that one, their leader—why did he just bow to me like that?"

"Oh, he weren't bowing to you," Jarrod replied with a mirthless chuckle. "I reckon they's just afeared of this here tunnel."

Turning, I scanned the encroaching darkness, shining my flashlight down the long hallway we were now trapped in. My first thought was to agree with him, yet I had no idea what could possibly frighten such a fierce race of terrifying assailants. As I peered into the depths of this mysterious subterranean shaft, I began to ascertain the characteristics of the enclosed environment which had just inadvertently saved our lives.

The tightly fitted stones making up its perfectly formed walls were all equally sized, featuring large, hand-carved bands of hieroglyphics running down both sides. Studying the designs, I noted they portrayed scenes relating to fertility rites and rituals. The images were quite stylized, but I could tell they represented our adversaries in various stages of procreation. There were human shaped pictographs displayed here as well, doing what could only be considered manual labor. Yet even though the carvings closely resembled the funerary adornments found in most ancient Egyptian tombs, I could tell they were not something left over from a bygone age. "I think we may have just discovered what happened to your townsfolk," I muttered as I studied the bands of hieroglyphs etched into the stone.

Whistling low through his teeth, the portly man ran his hand along one of the raised designs, considering them closely. "I do believe you're right," he said after a moment. Then, peering down to the other end of the hallway, he pointed. "Say, isn't that firelight I'm seeing down there? Guess maybe somethin's in here with us after all, and we just ain't met up with it yet. . ."

Glancing in that direction, I saw that the perfectly straight tunnel reached a turning point a few yards ahead of us. And at the end of this impressively built passage there was indeed a flickering glow of radiance leaking from around that farthest corner.

Starting forward, I moved toward this mysterious illumination, concern for our safety foremost in my thoughts. Whatever awaited us at the end of this curious, subterranean thoroughfare, I only hoped we'd be able to face up to it. So far, we'd been overmatched at every turn, and I had no further delusions that we could triumph in the face of such overwhelming odds. Yet Jarrod was still correct; we needed to act quickly and find another way around that exterior cavern. The longer Tunuhun remained a captive, the less likely it became that he'd survive. It was this thought more than anything else that drove me now. I had to find a way to save him, no matter how badly the odds were stacked against us. Taking a deep, calming breath and then releasing it, I moved toward this wavering light with a caution born from many years of stalking dangerous prey across the frozen arctic tundra.

When we reached the corner, I motioned for Jarrod to hold back as I crept up to peek around the edge. Beyond the bend was another long corridor, yet this one was lit by brass bowls filled with oil. These curious lamps were suspended on chains hanging from iron fixtures along the walls, and here the hieroglyphs adorning the well-dressed stone were carved with a more decorative aesthetic. Fanciful motifs that were perhaps meant to be soothing to the eye, if you were one of the inhabitants of this foul place, were prevalent on all sides. To me, however, the curling, semi-erotic pictographs were somehow deeply disturbing on a subconscious level. Whoever had created this place, it was not made for the eyes of man, and that much was imminently clear to me as I studied the repugnantly carved designs.

Turning away, I retreated to where Jarrod was waiting. "I thought you said these things were mere beasts," I whispered. "How could they have built all this, possessed the skills to construct these walls, to decorate in this fashion? Just what the hell is this place?"

"Well, now that I don't rightly know," he said ponderously. "I ain't never been down in these here tunnels afore. Had some friends a while back who done tried it, and that didn't end well for 'em. These here places, they's all filled with subservient beings, creatures who're beholden to other, more dangerous entities. Could be the powers controllin them things made some changes round here, changes I don't know nothin about. So, your guess is as good as mine when it comes to alla this stuff."

Staring at him, I wondered just what I'd gotten myself into with this maddened old fool. Yet he'd already proven himself to be an invaluable asset in navigating the hidden perils of this underground necropolis. I decided to give him the benefit of the doubt. "What was that device?" I asked. "The bright light you threw back there in the cavern?"

"Shucks," he said with a grin. "That weren't nothin special; just a lil 'ole magic trick. A bit of phosphorescence, some other stuff I done throwed together. Them type of critters, they don't like the light. So's I figured I'd give them a whole bunch of it to chew on whilst we was makin a break for it."

It was not the answer I'd expected, yet it spoke volumes about his inherent ingenuity. He had a more diverse range of talents than I'd previously given him credit for, or so it would seem. Shrugging away my reservations, I motioned for him to follow and then turned away, walking back down to the bend. Rounding the corner with my weapon leveled and ready to fire, I moved forward at a slow, easy pace. My intent was to search these corridors to see if they presented another means around the outer cavern that was currently filled with ghouls and hideous flying serpents. My mind rebelled when I thought of those repellent, snake-like entities, with their huge, leathery wings, unusually shaped snouts, and black, obsidian claws. I didn't have any idea what the hell they were, but felt no desire to get close enough to find out either. Moving down the hallway, which now strongly resembled the inside of an ancient pyramid, I sought for an exit while puzzling over the significance of this oddly placed series of hieroglyphically decorated passageways.

After a few moments, we came across doorways spaced at equal intervals to either side. They were framed by pieces of finely chiseled stone which were fitted together without any signs of mortar.

The blocks that made up this place were all so well-dressed and precisely cut that it struck me as odd to find this amount of architectural exactitude in a den of subhuman canids. I wondered if this could have been why the townsfolk were needed—for the building of these tunnels and perhaps others like them. Maybe, as it had been portrayed in those earlier pictographs, they'd all been forced into heavy labor in order to create these bizarre galleries. But that would infer that the canids dwelling here had a much higher level of intelligence than I'd previously imagined. No, this whole area was something else entirely, something intricately orchestrated by whoever was in command down here. The thought was less than reassuring.

Pausing by the nearest doorway on the left, I sidled up to the rectangular opening and then glanced within. Beyond the well-crafted frame of the door itself lay an immense room filled with low, stone platforms. More of the oil braziers were hung from decorative frames along the walls here, and a central pit hosted what appeared to be a coal burning fire, perhaps laid there to provide extra warmth. But what drew my immediate attention were the occupants of the low couches themselves. The entire chamber was filled with nude women, all of them quite human, and every one of them obviously pregnant. They lay in a state of mild stupor, their naked bodies glistening with sweat and oils, the rigidity of their distended abdomens gleaming in the flickering light of the wall-mounted lamps. As I stood there in shock, staring with my mouth hanging agape, they continued to writhe and moan softly, undulating sensually like a nest of torpid, well-fed vipers moving to some unknown internal rhythm.

"Looks like we done found the breeding chambers," Jarrod whispered, his moonish face gazing at the sight from over my right shoulder.

Giving it some thought, I decided that his assessment was probably correct. Yet what did it all mean? What were all of these women doing here and why were they so heavily pregnant? If there was a way I could save them, I knew that I would find it, but not now, not before we rescued Tunuhun. Swallowing the bile that rose in the back of my throat at the thought of leaving them to their fate for now, I motioned to Jarrod, and we began checking the other chambers along the hall. Room by room we worked our way forward, moving toward the far end where a massive statue rested between two decorative archways.

Each room was identical to the first, with writhing occupants resting upon low stone couches, yet I saw no attendants as we searched through these chambers of imposed pregnancy. Even so, I began to notice small injuries on the bodies of all the victims. There were bruises and contusions, partially healed abrasions, and bite marks. Quite a lot of bite marks actually, as if something had been nipping repetitively at their exposed flesh. The wounds were all mostly superficial, but that didn't make them any less disturbing. When I pointed it out to my companion, he just grunted in acknowledgment, his facial expression now cold and distant. Whatever had been done to these women, it didn't sit well with him either, and that much was certain. Without discussing it further, we continued on to the end of the hallway, both of us filled with a simmering anger and resentment that went well beyond the bounds of all rational thought.

The grotesque statue which stood at the culmination of this warren of misery and human suffering rested between two twin archways decorated in Egyptian motifs. It was quite large, reaching from floor to ceiling, and seemed to depict some sort of fertility goddess with her arms raised on high. The features of this loathsome deity were a mixture of canine and humanoid, a blend that was unsettling to behold on such a naked, female simulacrum. Even though it was clearly carved from richly marbled stone, it appeared entirely lifelike, its stout legs, heavy breasts, and distended belly all signs of irrefutable fecundity. However, its face was not like the other creatures we'd come across thus far. Instead, it was a blend of their characteristics, featuring wide, sensual lips and drooping, half-closed eyelids that gave it a sultry expression of sullen arousal.

This disgustingly unnatural mixture of human traits with the ghoulish aspects of the canids we'd already encountered was extremely unsettling. I felt chills running up and down my spine as I contemplated its obscene visage in the light of the oil lamps hanging from the walls around it. There was just something about it that struck me as profane, creating an aversion within me that I felt to the very core of my being. Tearing my eyes away, I slid to the left around the edge of the nearest archway and then moved cautiously into the adjoining chamber.

In this massive room there were no pregnant captives resting on couches. Instead, at the opposite end, laying on a tremendous slab of intricately carved marble and surrounded by colorful pillows, was a creature straight out of the depths of my darkest dreams. Long and distorted, this being lay among the strewn cushions, lounging in a position that completely exposed itself to our full examination as we stood gazing at it in dumbfounded amazement. It was definitely female, yet it was not this aspect of it that was so imminently horrific to behold. Its face, a mass of mixed human and canine elements, was somehow further deformed in such a way that it reminded me of those afflicted by the genetic disorder of neurofibromatosis. Huge, partially closed eyes were sunken within a lumpy skull rigid with protruding, flesh-covered cartilage, and its mouth, hanging half open, exposed row upon row of crooked, yellow fangs. Bristling hair sprouted in unkempt, sweaty ringlets across the rest of its ill-formed body, and the entirety of its astounding anatomy was proportioned like a gigantic snake who'd recently swallowed a caribou whole.

Yet none of this was even the most disturbing aspect of the unnatural scene now playing out before us. In addition to its other repellent features, it also had a multitude of flabby breasts running the entire length of it. And at these vile, swollen teats suckled dozens of small, ghoulish children, hairless bundles of spindly legs and arms, their bloated bellies filling with the sustenance this slug-like abortion of nature was providing. Without even realizing it, I'd taken a few more steps into the room, my legs working without my conscious volition, as I was drawn by morbid curiosity toward the unspeakable sight lying before me. Just what *was* this horrible thing? I did not know, yet could not tear my fascinated eyes away.

"This must be the whelping room," Jarrod whispered close to my ear.

Turning, I gazed at him in shock, realizing that he was right once again. This chamber and the rooms before it were all part of some hideous plan to raise these things, these human-ghoul hybrids. For what purpose I could scarcely fathom, but deep in my gut I knew it to be true. Searching the area, I tried to locate another way out, some hidden exit that we could perhaps use to leave this underground den of unnatural breeding, and it was then that I took in the further details of the chamber itself.

Colossal pillars rose at equally spaced intervals along the walls to either side, supporting a vaulted ceiling that was lost in shadows. And in between each of these pillars resided more of the lifelike statues depicting the fertility goddess we'd seen just outside the room. Yet these were all different from one another, each one more ghastly than the first, and all so realistically depicted that I felt my gorge rising just to gaze upon them. Thick, muscular arms, a massively proportioned chest, and rotund, tree-trunk sized legs seemed to be the only similarity between them all, the rest being a hodgepodge of distorted features riddled with a plethora of other unsightly deformities. It was enough to raise the hackles on the back of my neck as I stared in silent disgust, nausea clawing its way up from the pit of my stomach.

But as I stood there trying not to be overcome by a bout of uncontrollable vomiting, they began to move, coming at us from all sides across the vast expanse of this nightmarish, subterranean nursery.

6

These creatures, hybrids of animal lust and unwilling human participation, were humongous in size as well as terrifying to behold. Coming at us from all sides, they quickly had us restrained before we could even fire off a shot. Their loathsome claws bit into my shoulders and arms as I struggled against their superior strength, and I realized at that moment that we were going to die here. Our mission had failed. Tunuhun would be subjected to whatever horrors awaited him down that other passageway that we'd seen him being dragged off toward, and the book, a book which my uncle had entrusted to an utter madman, would be lost forever.

The faces of the monstrosities surrounding us were horridly malformed and repellent to behold. Ridges of cartilage jutted out from thick, sparsely-haired skulls that were conical in nature and vaguely dog-like. The eyes held no intelligence that I could see—just brutal predatory intent. As the creatures holding me grunted in their guttural, snarling anger, I could make out rows of needle-sharp fangs gaping wide to expose a long, blue-and-black tongue. With ropes of saliva drooling out onto me, the beasts which held me fast seemed to be fighting over who would get the first bite of my exposed head. Yet still I struggled on. Even knowing that I was not long for this world, the will to survive was a driving force that could not be quenched. Jerking my body back and forth in their iron-clad grip, I tried desperately to break free of their hold upon me.

"Ladies, please," came a rich, melodious voice from out of the shadows. "Is that anyway to treat our guests?"

At the sound of this cultured female voice, the things that were holding us captive stopped their salivating attempts to bite into my skull, going so quiet that I could discern clearly the sounds of the pups that were still suckling at the teats of the rotund creature that was lying on the whelping couch. My eyes searched the room around us, shock and horror intermixed within me as I sought out the source of this unexpected voice.

In the back corner of the room, there was an archway that I'd not noticed upon our arrival, most likely because these vile guardians had been standing in front of it at the time. As the creatures surrounding us who were not holding on to any of our limbs parted and then moved around behind us, I was able to clearly see that there was a dark presence standing in this entranceway. Shrouded in shadows, it moved forward into the light of the flickering flames.

Regal is the word that came to mind as I laid eyes on her, yet even that was an unfitting description for someone who was so elegant and also obviously in charge. My mouth hung open in shocked surprise as she glided farther into the room, and I found that I could not tear my eyes from her amazing appearance.

The clothing she wore was simplistic in nature, yet had a certain elegance all its own. Wrapped in layers that were colored in varying shades of blacks and grays, her attire reminded me of the Egyptian rulers of old. Her dress had panels that flowed down from her shoulders, which were beaded in onyx with intricate designs and motifs, while the undergarments covered much of her in a form-fitting wrap that left her shoulders and arms exposed. Her sandaled feet poked out from beneath the floor-length garment as she slid further into the room, and my eyes were drawn to her face, which was quite captivating under its elaborate headdress.

The golden headdress flared out from the top of her head like a widespread fan and was decorated in lapis lazuli, carnelian, calcite, and obsidian. This impressive crown also had flanges shaped like wings that swept down over her ears at each side of her head, and the face of an exquisitely carved vulture stared out at us from the front of the headband. I could see that there was cloth of gold ringing the back, and apart from that, the women appeared quite bald, without even eyebrows. Oh, but what a face it was. High cheekbones accentuated her coal-rimmed eyes, and the rest of her features were perfectly sculpted, with wide, expressive lips, a fine, straight nose, and buttery skin that was as smooth and soft-looking as the finest silk. But it was her eyes that drew my attention the most. They were jet black, without any pupils or sclera, and seemed to hold the wisdom of the ages. As she moved toward us, I felt my body betray me in unwilling arousal.

"Well," she said. "What do we have here then?" Stepping up to Jarrod, she ran one slender, perfectly shaped hand along his cheek. "You, we already know of. But this one," she purred, leaning so close to me that I could smell the cloves on her breath. "This one is new to us. Who are you, my ill-fated new friend? Who dares intrude upon the birthing chambers of Nitocris?"

I felt my face flush with embarrassment as my arousal became more pronounced. This woman was having an effect on me, and it was one that I didn't welcome right this second. We were in great danger, and I couldn't figure out how we would survive. Trapped here in these chambers that were filled with giant, malformed females and overseen by this stunningly attractive lady, there did not appear to be anything that I could say to talk my way out of a most certain death. But I had to try. Clearing my throat a little, I shifted slightly in an attempt to hide my now fully engorged erection.

"My name is Gillam," I said to her, meeting her eyes. "We did not mean to intrude; we were simply trying to find a way past the chamber outside of these rooms. Those things out there, they have my friend. And also a book that does not belong to them. We've come here to get them back and then return safely to the world above you. We mean you no harm."

She glanced pointedly at our weapons and then down at the bulge in the front of my pants. Her eyes roved over the contours of my body before she raised them to stare at me once more with an almost pleased-looking smile. "Your possessions betray your intent. You have come here, to these sacred chambers, armed and full of violence. And it seems that you are also armed with other, more tangible weapons." Reaching down, she stroked the front of my pants, and I felt a surge of passion roar through me. As I slid into a near swoon in heated reaction, she continued. "The penalty for invading my realm, these rooms in particular, is death. No male, not of any species, is allowed within these chambers, and for good reason. But, seeing as how you do intrigue me, I may yet let you live. But this one," she turned with a snarl on her lips, "this one will most certainly die! He has been a thorn in my master's side for far too long now!"

The look on Jarrod's face was one of glazed confusion. I could only guess that he was feeling the effects of the wondrous creature in a carnal way as well. His eyes bulged slightly while he sagged in the hold of his captors, the will to reply stolen from him by the passions that this queen was creating by her mere presence. Struggling against her powerful allure, I tried to focus, sought to distance myself from these unwanted feelings long enough to communicate with her. If I could only figure out what she wanted, who she was, perhaps, then maybe we could extricate ourselves from this precarious situation. Swallowing around the lump of desire that was stuck in the back of my throat, I tried to address her once more.

"We did not know that we were intruding," I said. "In fact, we have no knowledge of these rooms and simply wandered in here looking for a way out. Those creatures out there, the ones that have my friend, stole him from us along with the book. We're armed only because they attacked us first. All we know of this realm is that there are dangerous things living down here in the darkness, ghouls and who knows what else. We armed ourselves for protection, nothing more."

"Lies!" she hissed, her face clouding over with anger. "You have come here to kill, to wipe out any who stand before you. You are trespassers and will find no sanctuary here. The book belongs, has always belonged, to my master. It was never yours to take or possess. And now, it is ours once more, after hundreds of years. You will not take it back so easily. As far as the rest, these ghouls, as you call them, have lived here for centuries. This is a place of power, and one that draws many dangerous things to do its bidding. You have no rights here, none at all. And you would do well to consider that if you want to continue to live." Tuning to the hideous creatures which still held us, her tone became imperious. "Charity! Druella! Strip them of their weapons and then hold them fast. The rest of you, get back to your posts. Once the feeding time has ended, you will reassume your duties and take the infants back to the nursery. I will deal personally with these interlopers. And then, if you're very lucky, I will share what remains of them between you all."

There were grunts of assent and thinly-veiled passion from the rest of her companions as they moved with alacrity to obey her every command. We were quickly stripped of our weapons and patted down in a cursory way. Jarrod's pockets were emptied and were found to have a curious variety of objects, all of which these creatures stuffed into his already bulging rucksack. So much for his vast trove of magical objects; they seemed to have no effect on the things whatsoever. I was surprised at how nimble and dexterous these large and overly flabby servants were. Their fingers, long and strangely jointed, patted us down and emptied our pockets in a very efficient if not very thorough way. Our weapons were stacked on the floor and, as the others returned to their posts around the edges of the room, I stared up into the eyes of the thing that was holding me.

The exquisite creature that ruled here had called this one Charity, and she was the most repellent of the lot of them. Sagging flesh covered her grotesque face, making bags under her beady eyes and hanging in lard-filled jowls from her cheeks and chins. The sparse hair that covered her head was black and wiry, and her lips were wide yet barely covered the rows of ill-grown fangs. Her body was easily the largest and most disgusting of her compatriots, hung with rolls of sagging fat and ropy musculature. Years of breeding with multiple partners had left her belly a wreck, and it bulged over her midsection with the scarring of many stretchmarks. A more hideous sight I have never before seen. Staring into those eyes, I could tell that there was madness there, a desire to hurt, to tear and rend, with no inkling of compassion or other such soft, human emotions. As she caught me gazing at her, her thick, rubbery lips twisted up into a feral grin, and I knew then that she lived only to inflict pain upon others, that she took pleasure from dominating them and tearing them down until they were ground to dust at her feet. I would find no sympathy from this one, and of that I was certain.

As this loathsome nightmare took hold of me from behind once more, gripping me by my upper arms and pulling me back against her vile, fattened layers, I looked to see what the lady of this place was doing. Standing just a few feet in front of us, I noticed that her eyes were now fixated on the pile of my meager belongings. Seeking to determine what held her attention, I glanced down and studied the small pile of objects, yet could see nothing of any particular interest. There were my weapons, of course, and then a few odds and ends that any man might carry with him, but very little else. Then, I watched as she slowly bent down and retrieved the map fragment, the one that I'd carried since our misadventure in the Brooks Range. Straightening up, she turned the object over and over in her hands, viewing it from all angles.

"Where," she breathed in a soft voice, "did you get this?"

Her eyes rose to capture mine, and I felt a power roll through me. I was captivated by her glare and could only answer without prevarication. "It was found in a hidden base up by my village in Alaska," I told her truthfully. "The creatures there were from the stars and had just awoken from a long slumber, perhaps hundreds of thousands of years. I know not what they were, but we barely escaped with our lives. That fragment, it was in a room filled with photographic slabs, records of some kind, perhaps a history of their race as they were on their planet long ago. We believe that it may be part of a larger map, maybe an indication of other hidden places around the globe."

She looked at me, weighing my words. Although I knew that she would find no trace of untruth about what I'd said, it seemed that still she doubted my story as a whole. A puzzled frown crossed her delicate features, and her face grew grave with concern. Leaning back, she spread her arms wide, the panels of obsidian silk parting as they flowed from her bare shoulders. With her head thrown back, she began to chant, a sing-song voice filled with the power of the ages. A light sprang up, seeming to come from within her, and the crown on top of her head lit up with a fierce glow. I could see then that it was not only made from precious stones, but bits of wire and other electronic parts that had been so cleverly woven into its design that I had failed to notice them earlier. Yet now they became revealed as power rolled through her and the crown itself shone like a beacon in the night. In awe, I watched as ripples of energy sizzled through the wires and other electronic components of the headdress, illuminating it like the brightest star in a northern sky.

After a few moments of this chanting, I felt something enter the room, something that I could sense rather than see. Deep within me, fear blossomed, quickly becoming a raging inferno of terror that threatened to engulf me in an unbreakable grip of maddened, fight-or-flight response. Yet I could not move. I stood frozen, the horror of this monstrous presence filling all of my senses with a dread so vast that I could no longer function. Rooted to the spot in rigid immobility, my eyes darted around the room, seeking out the source of this all-consuming emotion. But there was nothing physically there, just a darkness that had invaded the place and now hovered about us like an unseen purveyor of mortal demise.

This monstrous entity of unseen threat swirled around the room, and I could feel it studying me, searching deep within the most hidden recesses of my very soul. A trembling started inside of me, shuddering outward and racking my body with uncontrollable fits and spasms of pure, unadulterated terror. Just when I thought that I could take no more, at the very brink of my mind cracking and my thoughts turning to utter madness, the presence abated, coiling itself around its chosen priestess here on earth. As it took ahold of her, she cried out in delight, her whole body writhing in sensual pleasure. If I wasn't already so scared that I was ready to pass out, I would have found her rhythmic motions almost obscenely arousing. And yet I stood with my mouth agape, trying desperately not to scream my lungs out and then fall into a mindless stupor.

Finally, after what seemed like hours, but was perhaps only minutes, her body ceased its unwholesome grinding and her head snapped up to face us. Her closed eyes slowly parted, and a wane light shone from them, like the shimmer of moonlight on water. Her arms came forward and down to slide along the curves of her tightly wrapped hips as she gazed at us in imperious disdain, and then her lips parted to utter a short, barking moan, like that of a lover captured in the last throes of an orgasm. She stood like that for a few moments, and then her eyes slowly closed once more, her chin falling to rest upon her delicate breastbone.

I stood transfixed, still held within the iron embrace of the foul thing that she had named Charity. I could not decide whether I should attempt to speak, or if I should await to see what happened next. In any event, I was in no condition to question this female conduit of eldritch energy. Experiencing this unholy event had told me much about the situation that I was now trapped in. Unlike the creatures we'd encountered in the great north, this presence that had inhabited her was far beyond anything that I'd ever encountered in the mortal realm. Its power was unquestionable, a tremendous evil that I had no delusions we could fight against. Here was an entity that was like unto a god, and I stood pale and trembling before it.

The beautiful lady's eyes finally parted again to stare out at us with the blackened normalcy that they'd shown earlier. This was not much of an improvement in terms of unsettling sights, but it was better than having whatever was once inhabiting her staring out at me. Swallowing the last vestiges of my primal fear, I gazed back at her, awaiting her next move.

Twisting her neck from side to side to unlimber it, she straightened her robes, her eyes never leaving my own. Then, she addressed our captors.

"Bring them," she commanded, "and all of their gear. The master would like a word with them below."

7

Without another word, she swept from the room, heading down the corridor in the direction we'd come from earlier. Her servants collected our things from the floor and then hastened after her, roughly shoving us before them like a couple of unruly schoolboys. I glanced over at Jarrod and saw that his rotund face was quivering with barely suppressed panic. As our eyes met for the briefest of moments, I could tell he was struggling to hold on to whatever remained of his already questionable sanity. Stripped of his arcane defenses, he had very little left to give in terms of helping us break free of our captors. Perhaps whatever awaited us below could be reasoned with, but at this point I didn't hold much hope that we'd be talking our way out of this. Racking my brain, I tried to devise a plan of action, but for the life of me I could not come up with anything that wouldn't result in our immediate demise. With despair in my heart, I continued following the queen of this unholy place toward whatever fate now awaited us.

We were escorted from the tunnels and across the main cavern where those flying creatures were nesting. They'd resumed their roosting in the shadows, but I could still see the points of their jagged wingtips jutting down as their bodies continually writhed across the rocky ceiling. In the glow of the phosphorescent plants, it made for a nauseating sight, a veritable mass of churning, serpentine forms heaving and squirming in the darkness above us. Tearing my eyes away from that unnerving spectacle, I focused on the priestess now leading us across this field of glowing fungi. What was it she'd called herself? 'Nitocris,' if I was remembering it correctly. I recognized it as having a definite historical significance, yet I could not recall the exact tidbit of information right at this moment. Sensing my interest, she turned to glance back at us, smiling with a small twist of her fulsome lips while gesturing to the flora around us.

"They're beautiful, are they not?" she inquired, indicating the many varieties of mushroom and other subterranean vegetation. "Before I came here, chambers like this one were filled with nothing but wild growth. None of it was ever harvested or tended to, and much was inadvertently trampled underfoot. Now that I'm in charge, it has been nurtured and cultivated into what you see here now. I have taught my minions to care for these plants, to train them into orderly rows. My leadership makes it so the creatures living here no longer rampage through these areas indiscriminately and allows us all to partake of this glorious bounty. These are my gardens, of which there are now many. Do you not find it tranquil and pleasing to the eye?"

Her speech put me more at ease, and I could feel much of my overpowering fear draining away. Now that she mentioned it, I did find them rather well tended to. Before, when we were on the ledge above this cavern, I'd thought it odd that all the ghouls had flowed through these fungi as though along paths instead of simply coming straight for us. It impressed me all over again with how much power this charismatic monarch had over the denizens of the nocturnal netherworld she now ruled. To keep such a race of hybrid mutants from defiling these areas must take a tremendous amount of painstaking control. My sense of awe at this woman's majestic powers shot up several more notches as I considered the sheer amount of effort involved in succeeding at such a monumental task. Seeking to ferret out more information, perhaps even obtain her favor, I attempted to draw out the conversation.

"They are quite beautiful," I said. "Yet, tell me, what are those things nesting above us? They attacked us earlier, but I don't recognize them as anything I've ever encountered before. Are they another hybrid of yours?"

Her laughter was like the soft tinkling of bells, melodic and sweet to the ear, and I felt myself unwillingly responding to her ever-present charms.

"No," she said, smiling radiantly. "They are my master's harriers, his interdimensional hounds. They are a servitor race, but not hybrids of anything as you or I would know them. He has many such beings at his beck and call. Soon you shall meet with him, be touched by him. Then you shall truly know the full extent of his awesome power. And when he is done with you, if you survive the madness that's sure to follow, I may yet take you for myself. You would know pleasures beyond your feeble five senses, pleasures you have never even dreamed of. I can give you that . . . that and much, much more."

My body responded strongly to her suggestion at the same time my mind was rebelling against the very thought of it. I would not be this goddess's plaything, no matter what she offered. Although I was intrigued by the possibility of exploring sensations beyond my current abilities, the idea also disgusted and scandalized me in equal measure. I didn't know what her ultimate goal was, but I knew I would do everything within my power to escape her clutches and then bring this hellish place crashing down around her ears. I just needed to figure out a way to do that while still rescuing Tunuhun and recovering the book.

"What have those other ghouls done with my friend?" I asked, hoping to change the subject. "Is he being taken to see your master as well?"

Her eyes grew hard as a small frown creased her glorious features. "Do not presume to toy with me!" she snapped. "I tantalize you with the promise of pleasures you can scarcely comprehend, yet you disregard my generous offer to inquire after your companion?" With a dark and sinister chuckle, she gestured around her. "These may be the last sights you shall ever see before you succumb to my master's desires. So look well and remember; I have offered to take you beyond what your meager five senses would allow, yet you spurned me in favor of mortal friendship. Well, it does me no harm to inform you that he is indeed below with my master now. But know this, and heed it well—his death will be a lengthy one, and we shall all sup of his lingering agony before the night is through!"'

With that, she turned away, heading for the elaborate doorway we'd seen Tunuhun being led toward earlier. So much for my ill-conceived attempt to garner her favor. With a sinking heart, I shuffled along, prodded by the grotesquery called Charity. Glancing about, I sought for a means of escape, anything we could use to break free of our captors. But I found nothing in the fungi-filled environment that gave me much hope of success. Instead, there were only rows upon rows of carefully tended plants and a ceiling crawling with the rustling movements of hundreds of leathery, bat-like serpents. With an air of defeat, I pushed forward, my hopes for survival dashed by our undeniably grim reality.

After a few minutes, we crossed in front of a large boulder covered in moss. Atop this ancient stone lay a particularly twisted and broken skeleton gone greenish-brown with age. I did not know who this person had been while they were still alive, but seeing the remains of another human being left to rot down here in these warrens did not inspire confidence within my already troubled mind. It was up to me to find a way to escape our captors, yet I had no idea how to initiate this seemingly impossible task. Would we wind up like this hapless individual, our bones left to molder here in these dank caverns for all eternity? Or would we be subjected to a far worse fate if I was unable to come up with a plan? With these bleak thoughts darkening my mood even further, I continued following Nitocris, my heart laying heavy within me.

When we finally approached the portal, I could see that it was well crafted, the lintel stones cleverly placed and fitted without any mortar. It put me in mind of the construction techniques used in the tombs of the great pharaohs. Studying it, I discovered there were many detailed hieroglyphics incised all around the framework, culminating in an elaborate symbol situated at its central apex. While I was staring at this complex glyph, I suddenly heard Jarrod give a low, throaty moan.

Turning, I witnessed him fall to his knees, his wide eyes filled with terrified recognition. "*Noooo—*" he howled, clutching at the ground and digging deep furrows through the rocky soil. "It can't be! We done banished him! We already done sent him straight back to the pits of Hell!"

The creature tending to Jarrod, Druella I think she'd been called, cuffed the back of his head and then grabbed his arms, dragging him to his feet as loose soil and debris trickled through his tightly-clenched fingers. Continuing his pathetic whimpering, he appeared to have succumbed to a bout of delirium, murmuring subvocal nonsense phrases and drooling as his captor got him moving once more.

I turned to see how Nitocris would respond to his outburst, yet she'd hardly noticed. Instead, she stood transfixed, her arms raised as she began another sing-song intonation in a foreign-sounding tongue. Before her, the darkness within the portal intensified while the imagery around the frame burst into sudden, eldritch illumination. There was something about the glowing, unfamiliar colors that set my teeth on edge, making the hairs on the back of my neck stand straight up. After a moment, the blackness congealed into a glimmering cataract, and she lowered her arms to continue forward through the now swirling accessway. Swallowing the gorge rising in the back of my throat, I followed her before Charity could shove me again. Whatever awaited us below, there was no sense in antagonizing our overseers by balking at this point. With that in mind, I decided to cooperate until I could figure a way out of this mess. With a grim sense of determination, I took a deep breath and then stepped into the obsidian darkness.

It was like being caught in a permeable barrier made of wet gelatin. For a few seconds, I couldn't even breathe, the panic within me threatening to overwhelm all of my other senses. As I moved slowly through this syrupy elasticity, the sensation of a thousand prickling needles rolled across my skin. But then, within a few paces, we were through and walking down a flight of stairs carved from the surrounding walls and adorned with wide mosaic tiles. These steps led downward in a spiral through a vast well that seemed to go on forever. The walls themselves were also covered in hieroglyphics here, and every few feet there was another set of those hanging lamps, much like the ones back in the birthing chambers. Yet these leaped with azure flames, causing huge shadows to expand and flow upward into the spaces above.

As we continued our descent, I tried to calculate how this stairwell could even exist within the series of caverns we'd just left. Moving down these impossible steps, I began to doubt my own sanity. By my estimation, there was no way this circular shaft could have been built within the common bedrock of the surrounding geographic region. Its massively constructed proportions and finely engraved motifs were much more suited to the burial chambers of fallen kings than to a festering warren of burrows hidden beneath an unnamed, North American town. The incongruity of it all continued to vex me as we followed the queen of these mysterious realms ever farther into its unknown depths.

After quite some time, we emerged onto a platform that was circular in nature, yet flagged like a Roman courtyard. Rubbing my aching legs, I stared at the sprawling vista now laid out before us. As I took in the panoramic view, my mouth hanging open in utter bewilderment, my hands slowly stopped their methodical massaging of my upper thighs.

If I'd thought the stairwell out of place, the spectacle before me was even more of a conundrum. Like a scene taken straight from a twisted fairy-tale, a cyclopean metropolis now rose before us. Huge buildings, minarets, and vast palatial estates covered an area which appeared to be limitless. Lit from above by an enormous disk that blazed from the center of the ceiling like a subterranean sun, this exotic and fantastical city was overflowing with archaic architecture ranging from across dozens of different time periods. Gardens, terraces, and fountains spraying delicate jets of water were also in evidence, and everywhere I looked there were amazingly intricate carvings of a twisted and gothic nature.

Not only that, but the streets themselves were choked with the citizens of this inexplicable place, the misbegotten souls of a truly twisted mind, the fruit of a thousand rapes and bespelled abductions—the ghoul-human hybrids.

Standing there gaping at this incredible sight, I soon became aware that the disk above us had begun to dim. Focusing my attention on this unexpected event, I was just in time to witness it pulsate, sending tendrils of energy coursing out along the multitudinous, interconnected lines surrounding it. This energy rippled from the central apparatus in waves of visible force, streaming through thousands of strategically positioned pathways that were routed in carefully planned patterns across an artificial sky. It reminded me of one gigantic circuitry schematic inlaid over the entirety of the cavernous ceiling. Trying to follow where these lines were being routed was pointless, but my eyes were drawn once more to the massive jumble of buildings and spires below it. All across this buried city of unfathomable origin, lights had begun to flicker and then hold steady as the entire collection of mismatched architecture lit up with an astounding array of iridescent coloration.

Like jewels placed upon a barbarous crown, the fantastical spires and minarets sparkled into life with glowing malevolence, showing me the denizens of this misbegotten world much too clearly for my own liking. There were crowds of misshapen canids everywhere I looked, their pale skin glistening and moon eyes glowing in the splendor of the gelid luminosity. But before I could do or say anything, the wretched horror that was my keeper shoved me roughly forward, grunting in satisfaction as I stumbled and fell to my knees upon the smooth, perfectly fitted flagstones. Crying out, I huddled there in abject misery, unable to stifle my reaction to the pain and the accompanying shock of being suddenly surrounded by hundreds of slavering carnivores.

Nitocris had stopped at the nearest balustrade, throwing her head back as she took in the view, reveling in all of its unnatural glory. Then, turning with a regal twist of her well-formed hips, she strolled toward me, her arms raised, with the palms held facing upward. Taking a stance just a few inches from my kneeling form, she gazed down, the allure of her heightened sexuality hitting me with all the force of a tropical storm. As I swayed beneath this renewed barrage of carnal desire and overwhelming lust, she laughed, her hands still raised in a travesty of benign supplication.

"What you see before you now is one of the greatest accomplishments of our lord and master," she said, emotion causing her voice to drop into sultry octaves that sent shivers coursing through my body. "The ultimate expression of the power he holds over life and death, even from beyond the worlds as we know them. This is the city of Gul'Nictolanthropep, and it is only the beginning of his carefully laid plans. So, take it all in, little man, and ponder upon this— my master will one day rule this planet and all who dwell within it. You would do well to heed his words when finally you meet." With that, she turned and glided away, motioning for our repellent guardians to hurry us along.

The beast named Charity dragged me to my feet and then shoved me forward. As the allure of Nitocris faded like the scent of perfume rapidly clearing from a ventilated room, I shook off the feelings of unwanted lust and followed this goddess of fertility, queen of unhallowed births and hybrid mutations. I knew not where she was leading us, but there was nothing I could do now but follow, my mind reeling from her presence and all I saw around us.

Risking a glance back at Jarrod, I saw that he was still mumbling to himself, perhaps a rambling prayer of some sort. With his hands clenched tightly against his chest, he shuffled along, eyes wide and unseeing. I almost envied his broken state of mind. I would have given much to be free from the fear and uncertainty I felt as I followed this cruel mistress deeper into the surrounding maze of interconnecting streets and byways. Seeing the immensity of this thriving community had filled my thoughts with unanswered questions, causing me ever-increasing levels of debilitating perplexity. Yet I still retained enough of my faculties to worry over what would happen should we meet the real power ruling here. I hoped for the chance of escape at the same time as I was considering a wide range of possible explanations for how this massive conglomeration of towering structures had come into being. Still, the answers stubbornly eluded my attempts at logical deduction as we plodded inexorably along.

Going by a circuitous route, we advanced through the hodgepodge of differing architecture, moving down cobbled streets past buildings of unimaginable size and function. Many of them resembled European cathedrals, dark, foreboding establishments decorated with elaborately embellished stonework. Yet none of the buildings we passed seemed to function like they would in the natural world, all of them housing large numbers of the artificially bred bipeds, yet in what capacity I could not determine. They were certainly not homes in any traditional sense of the word; that much was obvious just by observing the seething masses as they came and went through open doorways. A collection of overly large barracks, perhaps? It was hard to tell with any surety.

Studying the colossal structures as we moved along, I found that many combined techniques from the ancient Greeks, Romans, and Egyptians, while some were even the very epitome of modern-day aesthetics. Traveling through this tangle of gargantuan, highly stylized creations, I could not help but note the continued fluctuation of light from above us. Like electricity being shunted in bursts, the energy shot out sporadically from the centralized disk, passing along a complex series of carefully delineated conduits to somehow be drawn into the buildings themselves. From there, the power lit up thousands of sparkling bulbs and other luminescent devices, for what purpose or intent I could not possibly fathom. And the creatures here seemed to have acclimated to this unnatural brightness, their moonish eyes sparkling in the reflected radiance. It was all most peculiar. Lost in thought, I continued following Nitocris, moving through the twisted, well-paved streets in a daze of stupefied confusion.

After a while, we passed a series of areas nearer the edges of the city. There I saw large numbers of ghouls carving through solid rock with odd, handheld machinery. These devices cut huge blocks from the walls around them, some circular, some square or rectangular, then lifted these gigantic pieces of stone and either placed them into stacks for further use or disintegrated them into a fine, powdery dust. Was it possible that the city around us had been built by these creatures, a slave race forced into heavy labor for perhaps hundreds of years? It did not seem possible, yet it struck me then that here was the answer to our earlier riddle—with these machines, the ghouls could easily have cut through the cement foundation of Jarrod's shop. How they'd gotten past his spells, however, was still a mystery to me as we entered a centralized avenue leading up to a towering step pyramid located at the very center of this colossal, underground enclave.

Much like the ziggurats of Mesopotamia or the pyramids in Mesoamerica, this structure was a series of platforms placed in successively smaller layers and capped by a flat-topped pinnacle. The overall size of it was really quite daunting. Each of the sections was adorned with landings that contained cultivated plants arranged into beautiful gardens set just to either side of the wide, central steps. And the streams of electricity radiating outward from the disk in the sky seemed to culminate at the very top of this impressive construct. Searching the streets around us, I saw that the circuitry connecting all of the upper conduits formed complex designs overlaying the evenly spaced flagstones leading up to the monolith. Where did all this energy come from? What was it for and how was it produced? I had no idea, but felt sure that I was somehow about to find out.

Mounting the steps, our little procession continued up the wide stairway, moving at a slow, easy pace. As we shuffled along, climbing together, my eyes were drawn to the materials that had been used in creating this unusual monument, and I saw that the entire thing was made from a shimmering substance not unlike metal or some type of precious, semi-conductive stone. Above us, resting upon the summit, I could also now make out a cluster of oddly-shaped machines that reminded me of the relay stations located outside of heavily populated human settlements. These technological devices sizzled with power, energizing a wide array of illuminated control panels located just in front of them. Racking my brain, I tried to determine their purpose, but was unable to figure out what these electrical installations had to do with anything we'd seen thus far.

After an arduous climb that stole my breath away and was even more taxing on my flabby companion, we reached the very top of this artificial edifice and stood before a throne made of onyx and gold. Upon this throne, sitting with his legs crossed and hands resting lightly upon an upraised knee, was a man dressed in dusky robes, a decorative collar clasping his slender neck.

The features of his face were all perfectly proportioned, delicate even, his skin the deep, rich color of pure obsidian, yet not lustrous like normal flesh would be. I could see that he was completely bald without even eyebrows, much like his chosen queen, Nitocris. But it was the eyes which drew my unwavering consideration, as they were jet black and filled with tiny pinpoints of light, like stars scattered across a moonless sky.

The creatures guarding us dropped to their knees, bending low to the ground with outstretched arms in total subservient worship of this swarthy man who, to me, resembled nothing less than a wealthy Arab sheikh. After a deep bow of her own, Nitocris turned to us, waving a graceful hand back toward the ruler resting upon his elaborately constructed seat of power.

"On your knees, dogs!" she cried. "Bow before your one, true overlord, the Black Pharaoh, Master of a Thousand Forms, Nyarlathotep, Mighty Messenger of the Outer Gods!"

8

I didn't know what to think, how to react. What did one do when being introduced to a god? How could I even tell if this man was the deity Nitocris claimed him to be? Having no preexisting experience or knowledge to go off of, I stood transfixed, held immobile by a mixture of fear, awe, and indecision. It was difficult to stop myself from staring at the man's face, but I needed to buy myself some time to think. Therefore, I let my eyes slide away from him, gazing at the vast throne he rested upon, while trying not to be overawed by his obvious personal magnetism.

The device on which he sat was a massive contraption built of circuits and conduits all spliced together in an elegantly functional design. This conglomeration of electronics, sheathed in onyx panels and gold wiring, culminated in a large power cell serving as the backrest. Energy ebbed and flowed through its entire frame, yet its exact purpose was not immediately clear. Tracing the power conduits down to the smooth, semi-conductive surface beneath my feet, I saw that the lines radiating outward from this seat of sovereignty all led into the machines around us and then down the sides of the great pyramid itself. From there, they presumably ran back through the city, up the walls, and into the brass disk resting at the center of the artificial sky. I had no idea how it all worked, nor even why it did, but if I was being honest with myself, I found the whole thing to be immeasurably impressive.

Yet of Tunuhun there was no sign at all.

"Please," the man said, his richly-timbered voice flavored with a touch of mid-eastern accent, "these titles, they are so very formal and tiresome, do you not agree?" Rising from the throne, he stepped forward, the glow of the multitudinous lights shimmering around him as he came toward me. His robes were simple and similar to the ones Nitocris had on, yet beneath them was a finely-tailored suit with a high-collared shirt that buttoned across his slender neck. Much like his queen, all of the attire he wore was colored in shades of gray and black, but the panels hanging down from his shoulders were dagged and covered in golden embroidery, teasing my eyes with their intricately stitched patterns. "I am known by so many names in so many parts of the world now that it becomes rather difficult to keep track of them all,"' he continued. "The small-minded, plebeian residents of this backwater community simply called me Nathrotep. I would be very pleased, and honored, if you were to do the same. It will save us all a great deal of time and energy for surely you cannot be required to remember all of my titles if we are to successfully work together."

I caught a flash of movement from the corner of my eye, and saw that Nitocris had briefly recoiled in shock, startled by this unprecedented announcement. Swiftly recovering her aplomb, she inclined her head in regal acceptance, although clearly disapproving of its implications as a whole. Studying this outwardly cultured and well-spoken gentleman, I was uncertain of how to proceed. How did one even converse with such a cosmic entity? I quickly decided on directness; he was no god of mine, nor ever would be, so he had not yet earned the civility of my respect.

"What have you done with my friend?" I demanded. "And the book that you've stolen from us?"

His smile disappeared, like frost melting in the rays of the rising sun. "There is no need to be short with me," he murmured. "Good manners are never a waste of time. Your friend is in fine health and completely within my power, as you will soon discover. As for the book, well that was never yours to begin with. In fact, it was always mine to do with as I please, and as such, I have now reclaimed it as my own."

While speaking, he'd waved his arm in an expansive gesture toward Nitocris, and then stepped back to allow her access to a device sitting just to the left of the throne. It was much like the type of control panel you'd find at a power station, yet more finely crafted and elaborately designed. Levers and dials adorned the top surface, and there was even brass scroll work accentuating the other decorative elements inlaid across it in silver and gold. Like something out of the 1900s, this contraption was an artistic combination of refined engineering that I'd not seen anywhere else in all my many travels. With one slender hand, Nitocris maneuvered these controls, and then a panel in the floor slid open. From out of this newly formed hatch there arose a vertical metal rack which held Tunuhun immobilized in an upright position. Bound by golden bands at wrists, ankles, waist, and throat, he remained stationary as the flat, metallic slab slid upward and then locked into place, neatly closing the aperture where the trapdoor had once been. The whole process was smooth and seamless, as much a part of the colossal pyramid as everything else on this mind-boggling structure was. And on a small pedestal resting next to him was the book, waves of violet energy bathing it in ethereal light.

Seeing him there, strapped and bound like an animal being readied for the slaughter, I felt a boiling anger erupt within me. Knowing there was likely very little I could do at this point did not prevent the sudden urge to lash out, to destroy everything in my path in order to rescue my friend from this questionable god's diabolical restraints. Nathrotep must have seen the murderous rage spreading across my scowling features, but he only chuckled to himself, raising one hand in an open entreaty of forbearance.

"Now, now," he cautioned. "There is no need for such righteous indignation. I am merely keeping him safe while we discuss things rationally. It is unnecessary for you to be so aggrieved—surely you can see that he is alive and well cared for, at least for the time being. Come, let us talk, you and I. First and foremost, of course, you must explain to me why you've released the Mi-Go, and what you'd hoped to achieve by doing so. You may not realize it, but you, my friend, have initiated a chain of events that cannot possibly be undone. Because of your tiresome meddling, I have been forced to step up my own timetable in order to counter the threat of those bothersome fungi from Yuggoth. Do you not see how your actions may have been a bit incautious over the last few days? What you have done displeases me greatly. And yet here I am, willing to talk, willing to come to an arrangement of sorts. I will have need of servants such as yourself in the times to come, people with courage enough to claim their own place within the hierarchy arising from the ashes of your dying Earth."

My mind was spinning with the implication of his words even as my level of annoyance climbed to an even greater height within me. This self-proclaimed godling hoped to recruit me into his nefarious schemes? There was slim chance of that. Yet he already knew about those insect creatures we'd awakened, recognized what they were, perhaps even where they were from. Could I not use this information to my own advantage? Plans within plans spiraled through my mind, ideas and thoughts that went through rapid reevaluation the longer I considered them. There was one thing he'd not yet mentioned, something he'd left out that could possibly be in our favor. Those barrel-shaped beings Tunuhun had released, the ones I'd inadvertently developed a psychic link with—it was feasible that he didn't know of them yet. If I played my cards right, we could live to somehow make use of that information, could survive our current captivity while gaining more insight on the insectoids we'd already unwittingly unleashed.

But, even so, here was yet another existential threat, and one that was potentially greater than the possibility of an alien invasion. Whoever this Nathrotep was with all of his hybrid ghouls and odd machinery, he had to be stopped. This city, hidden beneath the earth and protected by this mad deity, could not be left unopposed. There had to be a way I could gain the information I needed to shut this place down before we escaped.

Seeking to judge my options more clearly, I glanced over at Tunuhun. He was bound, yet his eyes met my own with much the same calm composure he'd always shown. This man, this unflappable companion of mine, had more undeniable courage than I could ever hope to achieve. We made a good team, he and I, and I would not let him die here alone. He seemed to sense what I was thinking, for he nodded almost imperceptibly before speaking to me in our own language.

"Pisaasugluni. Ilitchugivlugu. Palaqtaqpaglugu!"

He was right; I needed to focus all of my efforts on becoming acquainted with this new adversary, and then use that knowledge to defeat him utterly. Once more, my trusted friend had seen clear to the heart of the matter. And he was willing to sacrifice his own life for the salvation of all mankind. With no thought for his own survival, he had spoken to me of what mattered most in this situation—we had to find a way to defeat this evil at any cost.

Nathrotep was smiling again, an expression of wry amusement gracing his swarthy features. "Ah, you speak in a language I am unfamiliar with. I do so hope that his words will encourage you to treat with me fairly. What I offer is no mere gambit to gain your cooperation; I can easily complete my goals without your help. But what a shame it would be to waste such a deliciously hearty resource. You see, my friend, you delight me to no end. Your resilience and stoicism in the face of almost certain doom is quite refreshing after all the mewling and pointless defiance I've endured from the many other lifeforms

I've dealt with over the ages. Yes, there is definitely something quite unique about you both. Even now, your minds resist the madness that is my especial gift to this fractious, mortal realm, a delirium caused by my mere presence alone wherever I choose to appear. Indeed, I find you to be quite intriguing. Are all of your people as steadfast in their mental fortitude as you two undeniably are?"

I had to steer him away from that topic. The threat was there, thinly veiled, yet obvious to me in all of its implications. My people would never fall for this ancient deity's obsequious manipulations, never be the earthly lieutenants in his fever dream of apocalyptic world domination. Not if I had anything to say about it. "Those creatures we've unleashed," I said, changing the subject, "what are they and where did they come from? We had no idea they were even there before the earthquake. Once inside their frozen hive, we were only able to determine they were perhaps thousands of years old, and that they had advanced technology we were unfamiliar with. I can assure you that our actions were never meant to unleash them at all. In fact, we did our best to destroy them and were hoping that the explosion of their base would finish them off. What will happen now that they've awakened, and what can we do to stop them?"

He reached out his hand, and Nitocris stepped forward, relinquishing the map tile fragment she'd taken from me back in the birthing chambers. For a long time, Nathrotep studied the object, focusing on the designs inscribed across its pale surface. Then he glanced up at me once more, a grin still tugging at the corners of his lips.

"A puzzle," he murmured, rubbing his long, agile fingers across the glyphs covering the slim piece of stone. "I do so love a good puzzle." His pitch-black eyes, flecked with the pinpoints of a thousand tiny stars, gazed at me intently as he continued, "This is indeed a partial map, as you may have already surmised. By following this and gathering together the rest of the fragments, or even finding another, more complete tablet with similar markings, you may yet discover additional Mi-Go facilities, uncover ways to defeat them, perhaps even obtain weapons to use against them in their upcoming bid to control your world. And this would all perfectly align with my own plans right now as well, for if I am to succeed, I will have to make sure that these intergalactic pests do not interfere. The ones you encountered are actually millions of years old and possess technology far beyond what you could ever dream of. They've been trapped here on this planet since before time began. Like many of the lesser forms of life, they have enemies, to be sure, and have fought countless battles across innumerable worlds, always conquering, always seeking to expand into new and more productive ecosystems. The ones you've released are but a fragment of the legions they can bring to bear against you if they succeed. But their world is quite distant, and the members of their race which have remained here throughout the long years are scattered. They stay mostly hidden now, acting only from behind the scenes, fighting amongst themselves from within occult organizations with opposing ideologies. Their own internecine struggles are the only thing that has kept them from enslaving the entire human race thus far, really."

Turning, he paced over to the right of the throne, gazing up at a globe churning with an internally lit, reddish-purple mist that hung suspended between two Tesla coils. As the crackling energy from the twin towers played along the surface of this orb, he mused aloud, watching the smokey substance trapped within swirl and pulsate. "My own plans are, of course, much more subtle. Yet they've required a great deal of careful preparation, and I would hate to see them go to waste. This city you are now standing in is but one of my many strongholds. With the power at my command, I keep it balanced here between the world of men and the worlds beyond, never fully a part of one nor the other. And as long as I hold my minions here, we are free to multiply without interference from the other powerful forces seeking to thwart my carefully orchestrated desires and beat me to the final prize."

"And what are your plans then?" I asked. "Just what is this 'prize' you speak of?"

He turned to me, his fingers still stroking the fragment we'd rescued from the Mi-Go base. "Why, to control this ball of mud that you pestilent humans refer to as the 'Earth.' To drive its inhabitants mad and then grind them back into the dirt they sprang from. To enslave all those who survive and ready this insipid world for the coming of the outer gods themselves. *The old ones were, the old ones are, and the old ones shall be again.* The time is now ripe for their coming ascension. Your governments are beyond corrupt, thanks in part to my own influence over these last few decades; people starve in the streets, and refugees run from one place to another, desperately fleeing their own morally bankrupt societies. With your current president here in the Americas my willing puppet, I have achieved the almost perfect environment to facilitate my return to the mortal realm. I had hoped to have more time to perfect the conditions which will make my second coming more impactful, but you have inadvertently moved up the timeline, so to speak. Now that the Mi-Go are involved, I must hurry to complete my own objectives before they can launch a full-scale attack, and my ghoul-human hybrids will be the unconquerable army with which I accomplish this task. And while I do appreciate the additional chaos that a Mi-Go invasion might bring, I would certainly not relish the competition. There can be only one Master here. Is that not right, Ezra?"

His attention had focused yet again on the mist-filled globe when he'd spoken these final words, and I could faintly hear a low, moaning cry coming from within it. Stepping away from the glowing sphere with a small chuckle, he moved to stand before me, gazing deeply into my eyes. For a moment, I was captivated, drawn into the abyss of his constellation-filled stare, drowning in mesmeric star fields, lost within the infinite worlds held captive inside those shimmering, ocular depths. Then the spell was broken as he grabbed my wrist, placing the map tile firmly into my open palm, and then closing my fingers around it. His touch was tingly and somewhat insubstantial, like being caressed by the spirits of the dead, and it sent shivers of revulsion surging along my nerve endings as my fist closed around the artifact.

This was absolute insanity. I'd thought finding a way to stop the prehistoric insectoids would be challenging enough. Yet I had not planned on being captured by an entity who was apparently a demonic deity from beyond interdimensional space. I needed to buy some time to figure out a way to oppose him, or at least somehow escape his clutches. "You can't seriously believe you'll conquer the world with a handful of corrupt officials and this army of defective ghouls," I said, attempting bravado. "More than half of all Americans own their own firearms and are willing to use them. We'd eat your pathetic army for breakfast in a matter of hours. And as far as weak, ineffectual presidents go, we've had that problem before and have always dealt with it by voting them out or impeachment. Your brainwashed puppet will have his strings cut sooner or later, even if he lasts until after the coming election. What will you do then, I wonder?"

His smile was brittle, yet he still appeared genuinely amused. "Ah, but these are just small parts of my overall strategy," he said, clasping his hands behind his back as he strolled to the edge of the plateau, gazing out over his subterranean city. "Do you know how long it takes an idea to disseminate across the planet from the moment of its conception to almost global recognition? Mere hours in most cases. Over 59 percent of your world's population now have access to the internet. Word of mouth takes care of the rest. And look around you." Turning, he spread his arms wide, indicating the machinery crowding the top of the grand pyramid. "Tell me, what do you see?"

I took a moment to study my surroundings more carefully, well aware that he was baiting me, hoping I'd be chagrined by whatever I deduced. And he wasn't wrong. Taking a closer look at everything atop this colossal monument, and at the various devices situated around his electrified throne, I realized that we were standing inside a massive central processing unit. What its purpose was, I wasn't entirely sure. But

I knew that it couldn't be good. "Are you suggesting that you control the internet?" I asked with no small amount of derision. "Even if that were possible, you still couldn't influence as many people as you claim. We're a lot smarter than you give us credit for."

"And there's where you'd be wrong," he said without rancor. "From here, I not only control the informational systems of your world, but I also influence everyone on the entire planet! Every computer, every cell phone, every tablet and laptop, including anything that can be controlled remotely, from drones to self-driving vehicles to weapons of mass destruction. Satellites, cameras, facial recognition, all databases linked to all devices everywhere, with full, unrestricted access to everything. You name it—*and I can control it!* And as far as your leaders are concerned, and the archaic system that you refer to as the 'democratic process,' we both know what a sham that is. Those few of you rich enough to buy their way in are the ones who really call all the shots. Besides, I have people well placed within all the various political parties, so no matter who's elected, *I win*. No one is safe from my whispers in the darkness. In fact, all of your kind would soon be wiping each other out if I gave them half the chance. Even without my influence guiding them, you Americans are beyond fanatical about your guns and gun ownership. But without a willingness to implement any sort of gun control at all, you have mass shootings, ethnic conflict, hate crimes, and even members of your own police force slaughtering innocent civilians. And all of these acts of gun-related violence are currently at a record high across the nation. It would appear that you humans positively thrive on killing each other off. The statistics don't lie, and that's not even counting the death toll from the nasty new plagues I've recently let loose. If I had more time, I'd just sit back and watch while most of your pathetic race either sickened and died or murdered each other over pointless arguments. After that, with my indisputable control of your computer technology and this ghoul hybrid army, I could simply stroll in and take over everything in less than a few hours. Given enough time, there wouldn't be enough of you left to even resist me at all."

His air of superiority was beginning to grate on my nerves. "If you could do that, you'd be in charge by now, even without these ghouls and all of our current political and virological problems," I said. "All you can really do from here is spread more chaos; no one's going to let you just override every computer system in the world—there's too many fail-safes in place for that. It's just not possible. Besides, if you really have all these human followers placed in high-ranking government offices, then why not just have them help you take over the world right now? Or even have Nitocris do all of your dirty work for you? What are you waiting for? If everything you say is true, then you don't need me at all. You could just let us walk out of here, and it wouldn't even slow you down."

"My plans are many and complex; I need not explain them to a mere human," he growled, his form suddenly growing taller than his lean frame would otherwise suggest. "But I will tell you this much, and it should be fairly obvious by now: I thrive on chaos. By definition, I am the very embodiment of utter madness and unrelenting fear. It is what I live for. To that effect, I've been slowly driving the population toward a mass extinction event over these last few decades while feeding on the anarchy I've created. Civil unrest, wars, famine, riots, racial tension, all caused in part by my carefully disseminated misinformation campaigns. So much violence, so much delicious insanity, that I can hardly even contain myself!"

Pausing, he clasped his hands together, tenting his index fingers while staring at me with amusement crinkling the edges of his darkly glowing eyes. "My followers on the surface are legion, yet they all lack a certain initiative and willpower, which will be crucial to controlling my forces during the second coming. They will serve me well enough, but I would not trust them to maintain discipline afterward. Their infinitesimal intellects could not possibly handle the raw power required to resist the madness of my personal presence once it stands before them in the flesh. Nitocris is my Queen, resurrected to be the mother of all my children, the fertility goddess of my breeding farms here on Earth, yet nothing more. *You*, on the other hand," he said, pointing at me with one long, finely-boned finger, "you have the resilience and the tenacity to see that my armies will prevail, to make sure of the remaining population's willing capitulation once I've swept the field clean of those few left who'd dare to oppose me. Even now, I can sense that you're planning to try and thwart me. At the very first chance you get, I can tell you will do everything in your power to defy me and see all my carefully formulated plans laid to waste. The fact that you can even resist me now is in and of itself no small feat; I will need that willfulness, that intuitive disregard for the madness I bring, in order to have a competent herald who can make his own decisions without my constant supervision. And your defiance is so very refreshing, a new challenge for me to overcome, something that will give me much enjoyment as I satiate my curiosity of your unusually resilient mind. Yet, hear me now and heed well this dire warning," he said, flinging his other arm out to point back at the globe filled with swirling, reddish-purple smoke internally lit by its own hellish amber glow. "Others have sought to defy me, but all have failed miserably. And they have suffered greatly for it. Isn't that right, Ezra?"

A sudden eruption of movement in the air above the pyramid drew my attention as a group of the coiling, winged serpents from the outer caverns exploded into existence, swarming around the orb, and snapping at it with their sharp, irregular teeth. From inside of that mystic sphere there came a sudden, maddening shriek. It was enough to make me take an involuntary step back in an attempt to distance myself from this unexpected, bone-chilling altercation.

With the lights in the chamber dimming, and his hunting horrors gyrating through the air above him, Nathrotep's slender frame took on a far more sinister aspect. Gone was the false benevolence, and behind him, rising up out of the gathering shadows, I saw the outline of his true form, a huge, three-legged behemoth with a writhing throat tentacle in place of a head. Blanching in pure, unadulterated terror, I took another step backward, and felt the heel of my boot strike up against something. Glancing down, I noticed that the pile of our belongings was right behind me now, and saw that I'd came to a stop next to Jarrod who was still mumbling subvocal nonsense, his eyes wide and unseeing.

"You *will* serve me," Nathrotep intoned, "or you will *die*! Make your choice; it matters not to me! Either way, I will succeed! And the old ones shall reign upon this world once more!"

Nitocris looked shaken, her coal-black, pupil-less eyes darting back and forth between me and her lord and master while the two ogre-ghouls continued to lay face down in supplication, sobbing in uncontrollable fear. As the backrest of his royal throne pulsated with supercharged particles of endlessly collected energy and the lights around us dimmed even further, I focused on the technology covering this subterranean, tier-stepped plateau. In its darkly gathering power I saw the beginning of the end for all life as we knew it, an extinction event contained within the inner workings of this mad god's doomsday device.

There was nothing I could do to stop it, and my mind nearly ruptured as I glanced back at the demon towering above me in the swirling shadows, knowing with utter certainty that I would die here alone and unmourned.

9

The power swirled across the top of the pyramid, a veritable cyclone charged with vibrant electricity, and I felt my hair rise up, responding to its lightening-induced touch. In an attempt to comprehend what was going on, I forced myself to watch the spectacle unfolding before me. Nathrotep stood at the very center of the gathering storm, raising his arms as the machinery pumped the collected energy into his throne, then out through his body, and finally into the air around us. Because of this increased level of activity, the infernal device was now glowing white hot, like a beacon of oncoming doom set against the backdrop of his unfathomable desires. And in the orb behind him, the smokey essence of his once-faithful minion continued to wail and gibber, its pulses of interior illumination flaring against the prison of glass with ever increasing bellicosity. As Nitocris fell to her knees, gazing at her lord and master with a reverent expression, I knew in that moment that our lives were most certainly forfeit.

"Make your choice!" Nathrotep intoned, his voice a hollow, sonic boom that throbbed through the air with an echoing resonance. "Either serve me now as the commander of my indomitable ghoul legions, or taste the unchained fury of my all-encompassing wrath!"

I wasn't sure what to do. Choosing between becoming the willing servant of his madness or dying here now in a show of pointless defiance was really no choice at all. Death would be preferable, although I did not want to end my life here, did not want to fail in our mission to save the planet from being enslaved and destroyed.

The things we'd unleashed from their frozen sleep in the mountains of the Brooks Range had been bad enough, but here was an unholy enemy that was an even greater threat. What was an alien invasion when compared to the plans of an insane demigod with the ability to override all of our computers on a whim? With the merest thought, this being born of chaos and strengthened by the misguided desires of ignorant souls everywhere could entirely annihilate us. The world would become a wasteland as the technological systems he controlled killed millions with weapons designed to work with those very same programs. We would be utterly undone.

However, before I could form a coherent reply to his ultimatum, Jarrod rose from where he'd been kneeling, his mumbled prayer growing stronger as it burst from his slobbering lips in a foreign-sounding rhythm. His fists, still clenched tightly before his chest, started vibrating as a pale glimmer of light suffused them. Then, like flower petals opening to the morning sun, his fingers unfurled, releasing a collection of rocks and debris that he'd been holding since falling to the ground outside of this hellish underground metropolis. Flying from his hands at high velocity, these particles, energized by the spell he'd been surreptitiously weaving, shot straight toward the mad god standing before us.

But rather than striking Nathrotep down, they passed through him as if he were a ghost, colliding with the glowing orb instead, and shattering it into a million pieces. The churning remnants of his once-loyal servant, now freed from age-old captivity, swirled through the open air, luxuriating in its newfound freedom. Then, gibbering with malicious intent, the spirit made a beeline toward the closet living target. I could do nothing to intervene as the undulating, vaporous entity surrounded the now struggling Tunuhun, seeping through his pores and trailing dark essences down into his most vulnerable cavities.

Stiffening, Tunuhun fought against this brutal invasion of his innermost self, closing his eyes and trembling in unimaginable agony as Ezra violated him. But within seconds, his eyes snapped back open, now misted over with a blood-red sheen, and a triumphant grin spread across his still quivering features. "At last!" an unfamiliar voice croaked from his lips, "I am finally free!"

With a series of sharply uttered syllables, the spirit shattered the bonds holding Tunuhun imprisoned and then reached out to pluck the book from within its protective field. Once he had this worm-eaten tome in his possession, he stepped from the metallic platform, quickly scanning the dust-filled pages while his expression brimmed with feverish intensity. Raising one hand on high, he then began to chant in a crude dialect which I found incomprehensible, yet seemed all too familiar to Nathrotep and his queen.

Climbing to her feet, Nitocris raised her own arms, calling out in a sing-song voice to the serpentine minions who flew in gyrating circles above us. But without pausing in his recitation, the spirit controlling Tunuhun lowered his arm, and a powerful blast of energy shot out from his open palm. This amber-colored ray of crackling illumination hit Nitocris full on, causing her to crash backward into the throne, the hunting horrors above her crumbling into dust as they sizzled beneath the beam's ferocious onslaught. Seeing this, Nathrotep howled in protest, the image of his true form looming larger in the shadows behind him.

But then, Jarrod suddenly joined in on the spirit's droning chant, his shouted syllables matching those of the released warlock, and their vocal refrain combined into an unrelenting cadence. The spell they were weaving, now made more powerful by their entwined voices, coalesced into a cloud of undulating ripples, much like heat waves shimmering in the desert sun. Encapsulated within his whirling, electromagnetic storm, Nathrotep snarled, continuing to manipulate the throne's energies while the throat tentacle of his interdimensional shadow lashed through the air with ever increasing substantiality.

"You fools!" he cried, his voice booming out over their echoing chant. "You think your petty incantations can bind me? Do you really believe you can succeed? Ha! You merely prolong the inevitable! I am the Master here! *And. You. Shall. Not. Prevail.*"

Thrusting his arms upward, he wove his hands in intricate, mystical patterns, his thunderous voice overriding their vibrant intonations. Dazzling colors held within matrices of glowing astral configurations filled the air as he worked, the machines sparking and sizzling while the onyx throne continuously filled him with an unlimited supply of esoteric power.

With his attention now focused elsewhere, it inadvertently gave me the chance to act. In desperation, I knelt and dug frantically through our small pile of belongings, my hands finally closing around the shotgun, a powerful weapon made specifically for military combat. Climbing back to my feet, I shot the two ogre-ghouls first, blowing their disgusting, malshapen heads into exploding chunks of blood-soaked pulp before they could rise again and attack. Then, stepping over their quivering remains, I aimed for the throne itself. Round after round I blasted into that mechanical abomination, until it finally exploded into white-hot shards of smoking electronic debris.

Nathrotep turned his star-flecked gaze upon me then, his insubstantial form depolarizing as it began to fragment. While he blurred in and out of focus, losing resolution by the second, he glared at me, his frightening visage filled with the promises of forthcoming retribution. Then, without another word, he faded from sight, leaving behind only a terrifying afterimage that was burned across my retinas like I'd been staring too long at the sun. Rubbing the tears from my eyes, I blinked away this visual anomaly and then glanced around, trying to determine the outcome of the throne's total destruction.

Above us all, the shimmering brass disk at the center of the artificial sky fluctuated, wavered, and then went out, casting the whole of the underground cavern into a semi-darkness, broken only by the flickering glow of lights still charged with residual energy. From the depths of this shadowy hellscape there then came the howling of a thousand canid voices lamenting the dissolution of their foul deity, a maddening sound that filled me full of unspeakable dread.

But Nathrotep was not truly defeated; I knew we'd only postponed his physical appearance in our dimension for the time being. With all the power he'd accumulated, and this innumerable army of hybrid ghouls, he was still a force to be reckoned with. Shaking my head, I decided that now was not the time to worry about what he would do next. Instead of dwelling on things that were currently beyond our control, we needed to focus on escaping this subterranean necropolis before it fully destabilized.

Jarrod had stopped chanting when the spirit fell silent, but he still stood rooted to the spot, staring in horror at the red-eyed creature that my companion had become. Clapping him on the shoulder, I motioned toward Tunuhun. "Gather up what you can carry and then grab him," I shouted over the wailing of the oncoming hordes. "We need to get the hell out of here before we're overwhelmed!" Without waiting for his reaction, I turned and fired my weapon into the first glut of ghouls clambering over the edge of the pyramid, blasting the forerunners back into their companions and causing a huge tangle of howling bodies to tumble backward down the steps.

I knew we had to somehow make our escape without being torn apart by these vengeance-seeking carnivores, and so I moved to the top of the stairway, staring out over the city while accessing our options. The vast metropolis was now beginning to fade in some sectors, a lot of the buildings taking on a wispy, ethereal look. Seeing this, I realized we had to act fast or risk being pulled along with it back into the nether regions of interdimensional space.

As I stood shaking in fearful indecision, the ghouls regrouped on the landing below me, snarling as they slowly regained their courage. And down in the streets, I saw hundreds more pushing in toward our position, thronging every avenue and clogging the alleyways in a maddened rush to tear us limb from limb. Their bodies, crowded together in such capacity, took on the resemblance of one gigantic organism, a titanic creature made from flailing limbs and gnashing, razor-sharp teeth. In a near panic, I scanned the view to either side, but it was as I'd feared—all the streets were packed with enraged ghouls, their sinewy bodies converging on us from every direction. Glancing back over to Jarrod, I saw he was jamming his pockets full of gear and gathering up the rest of our belongings as quickly as he could while still staring at Tunuhun with a scowl darkening his flabby features.

Tearing his eyes away from the spirit, who stood motionless as if gripped in some kind of internal struggle, he glared at me. "I ain't helpin that thing!" he raged. "He's the reason we got inta all 'o this mess in the first place!" Turning back, he jabbed a thick forefinger in its direction. "Ezra Jeddidiah, you black-mouthed sonovabitch!'" he shouted. "You can just go back an rot in whatever foul hell done spawned you for all I care!"

He wasn't making much sense, especially given the fact that the two of them had just been working so well together on a spell from that book of his. But one thing was certain now; he knew the spirit that inhabited Tunuhun's body and wanted nothing more to do with it. Hoping to avoid an argument, I grabbed his arm to shake some sense into him. "Look around you!" I cried. "We're about to be overrun! This is no time for debate; we need that damn book, and I'm not leaving Tunuhun behind! So grab him and let's go—we can figure out a way to get rid of the spirit later!"

Jarrod's mouth opened, his chin moving as if he were trying to find a compelling reason to reject my heated command. But then, glancing around, he saw the danger we were in and made a difficult decision. "Awright," he agreed reluctantly. "But don't says as I didn't warn you."

It wasn't a total capitulation, but it would have to do for now. Turning, I stared at Tunuhun, trying to see if there was even a spark left of my old friend residing within those madly-glowing eyes. But the thing now wearing him like a second skin showed no sign of anything even remotely familiar—just an unrecognizable expression of purely fanatical glee.

With this deranged look still plastered across his face, he suddenly came to life, striding forward and shoving me out of the way before stopping at the very edge of the platform. Then his insane laughter boomed out across the darkened city, echoing from the remaining rooftops. "I am free at last!" he crowed.

"And now *I* am the Master here! Taste of my rage and tremble before me, you ungrateful dogs!"

Cradling the book in one arm like a mother holding an infant child, his free hand shot out as he began chanting again. Power rippled through him, traveling down his arm and gathering along his outstretched fingers until it coalesced into a strobe of energy which blazed forth in a wide, amber-colored beam. As this sizzling ray of eldritch power blasted its way down the wide, central steps and then out through the crowded streets, everything it touched was turned to a foul-smelling ash. From below, there came the fever-pitched screaming of thousands of creatures being brutally incinerated, trapped in place and unable to escape due to the tightly-packed crowds jamming in behind them. Soon the avenues and byways in front of the pyramid were clear once more, the ghouls in this area having been completely annihilated.

Swallowing my nausea and covering my nose against the abysmal stench, I grabbed Tunuhun, who was standing lost once more in an internal struggle against the invading spirit, and prepared to make a run for it. But as we readied ourselves to flee, I noticed that Nitocris had stirred from her unconscious state and was climbing unsteadily back to her feet. However, there was no time to deal with that now, and so we ran, seeking the tenuous safety of the darkened maze below us.

Upon reaching the bottom of the wide steps, Jarrod skidded to a halt. "Where to now?" he shouted. "How the hell do you suppose we're gonna get outta this place afore it disappears?"

It was a good question, but for once I had a plan. Using a flashlight to guide us, I angled down an alleyway, making for the area once filled with hybrid construction workers. Upon reaching this now deserted location I picked up one of the discarded machines from where they'd been left in a heap upon the dusty ground.

The controls were simple enough, being made for the lowest form of ghoul that lived in this accursed place, and so I pointed the mechanism, which resembled a cross between a weed-whacker and a vacuum cleaner, at the nearest wall, toggling the large red switch on the handle. Unsurprisingly, a beam of energy shot out and began immediately vaporizing the stone, melting it away and forming a smooth-sided tunnel.

With the power of Nathrotep negated, and his gigantic, centralized computer-core of a city fading back into the realm from whence it came, the barriers between our world and the next were sure to be thin. Or so I hoped as I bore us a pathway angling upward. I only glanced back once as we fled into this newly formed tunnel, and it was then that I saw Nitocris standing tall at the apex of the pyramid, backlit by the malfunctioning machines, with her arms outstretched to the artificial sky. Her eyes were ablaze as great multitudes of the remaining hybrid creatures clustered around her, and then, at her command, they came swarming down the central steps in an unending sea of fangs, claws, and glowing, moon-shaped eyes. With a small cry of despair, I turned back to my shaping of the tunnel, hoping against all odds that we'd make it out of this chamber alive before we were swept away under an oncoming tide of feral, carnivorous death.

10

The machine in my hands vibrated as I cut through the hard-packed earth and rock that made up the foundation of the unnamed town. Much like a jackhammer, it was difficult to control, and my arms trembled from the strain of holding it steady. Behind us, I could hear the maddened howling of the ghouls as they got closer, following our path in a mass exodus from their rapidly dwindling sanctuary, a race of misbegotten beings who were now hot for our blood.

"Y'all best hurry up!" Jarrod shouted over the noise of the cutting tool. "Them critters is getting mighty close now, and they's not gonna stop 'til they catch us!"

"Thanks for stating the obvious," I yelled back, too shaken to be tactful. "Why don't you try doing something about it before they get here? I'm going as fast as I can!"

"Oh, I think I can manage a few small tricks," the thing controlling Tunuhun's body said. "I don't know who you two gentlemen are, but these filthy jackals are well known to me, and they've earned their damnation a thousand times over!"

I couldn't turn to look back at what the spirit was about to do, but I thought I heard him start chanting again, his guttural vocalizations sounding odd coming from the mouth of a man who so rarely spoke aloud. Shaking my head in wonder at the situation I now found myself in, I pressed forward, cutting the earth and rock from our path with single-minded determination. If we could just make it to the surface, then maybe we'd have a chance. What kind of a chance we'd have against the hundreds of ghouls still pursuing us, I had not a clue. Yet the will to survive was strong within me, and the experience I'd gained while on dangerous hunts in the past had taught me to persevere while maintaining a level head. There was no use in panicking; that would only expedite our almost-certain demise.

Taking a deep breath to steady my nerves, I continued to aim the uncanny device at the wall of stone in front of us, cutting upward at an astonishing rate of speed and pressing forward into the freshly excavated sections as the tunnel lengthened. I felt rather than saw the effects of the spell the spirit was casting, a tingling up and down my spine as the hair on the back of my neck stood on end. The sizzle of roasting meat followed, accompanied by the screams of creatures dying en masse. Focusing on the job at hand, I ignored the awful sounds and the foul odor of burning flesh, my stomach roiling as I pushed forward, carving a path I hoped would lead us to safety.

But, after only a couple more steps, the device suddenly sputtered, coughed like an engine backfiring, and then went dead in my hands. Whether it had run out of energy or had gotten deactivated in some other way, I did not know, but it was now utterly useless in our attempted escape. Dropping the machine, I turned, my eyes scanning the spell-lit corridor behind me.

Jarrod was crouching at my feet, his arms covering his head, the act of a true coward who'd already given up on living, while before him the spirit stood braced in the center of the tunnel, glowing as he read aloud from the book clutched in Tunuhun's large, capable hands. Beyond them both was a nightmare scene that made me shudder uncontrollably, fear rocketing through my body and triggering my flight-or-fight instincts as I took an involuntary step backward.

From wall to wall, the circular corridor was packed with the hideous members of Nathrotep's hybrid army, scuttling over every surface and covering the entire rough-hewn shaft in a tide of corpse-colored flesh. Even as I hastily retrieved the shotgun from where I'd slung it across my back, they surged forward, howling with enough bloodlust to make me want to flee in terror. Yet there was no place left to run. Here beneath the soil of this foul, godforsaken place, we had dug our own final resting place, a testament to our failure at winning free from Nathrotep and his reincarnated queen, Nitocris.

Banishing those morbid thoughts from my mind, I opened fire, the bullets from my weapon tearing into the oncoming crowd as words of power ripped from Tunuhun's bespelled throat, the ancient spirit casting forth deadly passages read from my uncle's archaic book. But our concentrated, dual attack did little more than push back the raging tide of destruction as the creatures simply pressed forward over their fallen comrades. Even the warlock's spells were having less effect this time around, as if his strength was somehow waning. It was a losing battle, but I was not about to give up. Screaming into the faces of the advancing horde, I defied them, unwilling to go quietly into the oblivion of our impending death.

A terrible wrench of shuddering earth suddenly interrupted the battle, and there came a palpable change to the atmosphere of the tunnel, a rippling twist in the very fabric of time and space itself. Wailing in protest, the entire ghoul-filled section suddenly dematerialized as their fading city was sucked back into the dimension from whence it came, leaving us with a wall of unbroken stone where the enemy-packed corridor had just been. In the resulting silence, only the sounds of our heavy breathing, the sobs of Jarrod, and the trickling clatter of loose pebbles were still evident.

When I'd destroyed Nathrotep's throne, I must have interrupted the link he'd formed with the entire underground complex. His power here was broken, and it had therefore retracted his interdimensional pocket of space back into whatever plane of existence it had originally came from. The very thing that he'd wrought to protect his hidden city had ultimately led to its undoing. By making the place a separate universe suspended between our reality and the next, he'd shielded it from outside influences, yet had never planned on having anyone confront him from within its very confines. But I was no fool; I knew that this was only a temporary setback for a being of such great power. The colossal cavern with all of its archaic buildings and strange, electronic machinery still existed somewhere, perhaps in a place where he still had as much control over it as he ever did here in my own dimension. No, I was quite certain that he would return, and most likely he'd be ready for us the next time we met. It was inevitable.

For now, though, we were faced with another dilemma. This tunnel fragment was only a fractured segment left over when the edge of this other reality had been cut off from our world. With a limited supply of air and nothing to help us dig our way out, we would soon perish here from lack of oxygen. Peering through the gloom, I tried to penetrate the darkness now surrounding us, attempting to take stock of the situation and analyze our options.

From the ground at my feet came the sounds of someone digging through a rucksack, then light suddenly bloomed as Jarrod activated a portable lantern. In the illumination of its battery-powered LEDs, the interior of the blocked tunnel took shape around us, showing me that Tunuhun, or rather the creature who now controlled him, was standing right next to me, an insane grin writ large across his stolen features. As I studied this ancient warlock released from the globe where Nathrotep had kept him imprisoned, I wondered just who the hell he really was, and where precisely he'd come from.

His deranged facial expression was starkly shadowed in the lantern's light, his eyes a gleam of shimmering redness, watching me, while his lips were stretched in that unnatural rictus I'd never seen before on the face of my friend. With Tunuhun's long, black hair plastered down by sweat, and his muscles bulging from beneath badly torn clothing, he looked like a parody of the man I knew so well. The sight of it was extremely unnerving.

Jarrod stood, dragging his rifle up with him, and then aimed it at the demented spirit. Without thinking, I snatched it out of his hand, glaring at him. "What the hell do you think you're doing?" I demanded. "You can't shoot him! He's my friend!"

"In case you hadn't noticed," Jarrod shot back, "that *thing* ain't your friend no longer! That there's Ezra Jedidiah, or what's left of 'im, and his family's been makin this whole damn area a livin nightmare ever since they showed up near a hunnert years ago. Them people was crazier than the mad hatter, and they built themselves a cult that's lasted throughout the ages. Fact is, around thirty years back, it were Ezra and his disciples that just about succeeded in allowin Nathrotep to come through to our world in the flesh, right here 'neath this very town! If it weren't for a couple of people that used to live round these parts takin him on at the time, he would've succeeded too! But we stopped him then, and ever time since that he's tried. It were only in the last few years that this here bastard's been missin, most likely when he got imprisoned for failin his blasted god over an over again! It were about time he got his comeuppance, but now that he's free and in control of a new body, we gots to kill him, and be right quick about it, or there'll be all hell to pay!"

"There must be some other way to get Ezra out of Tunuhun, some spell in that book!" I cried. "We can't give up; my friend is still in there, still alive! There has to be some other solution besides just killing him!"

"Gentlemen, please," Ezra interjected. "There is no need for further argument; I am through being Nathrotep's plaything. Spending time being tormented inside of that fucking globe has shown me the error of my ways. Now that I have a new body, I plan on using it for a greater purpose. I will no longer serve a master that can never be satisfied; it is an exercise in pure futility."

I stared, my mouth hanging open in surprise. After taking a moment to gather my wits, I tried to reason with him. "But you can't stay inside of Tunuhun; we need him back. There must be some other way for you to continue on without him. Surely we can come to some sort of accommodation?"

"You can't bargain with that thing!" Jarrod exploded. "He's the ancient spirit of an undead necromancer! We can't trust anythin he says! The only thing we can do now is kill him, and right quick, before he can use that damn book to do somethin horrible to us both. You gots to listen to me! It's either him or us now!"

"I grow bored with your petty carping," the spirit said, lifting his hand to point at us with glowing fingertips. "*Shokk!*"

Diving out of the way, Jarrod and I both hit the floor to either side as a stream of light shot from Tunuhun's hand, striking the wall behind us and melting straight through it. With a rumble, the sloping tunnel collapsed in that area, showering us with dirt and debris as the end of the corridor crumbled, disintegrating before our eyes. As the dust settled, I could see light leaking through the large hole he'd created.

"Now, if you gentlemen will excuse me," he said, a feral grin nearly splitting his face in two, "I have better things to do than stand around here arguing."

Strolling between us, he made for this newly formed exit without even a backward glance. Yet, as he crossed in front of me, I reached out, grabbing his arm.

"I can't let you leave," I said. "Tunuhun's body is not yours to take, and I will fight you with every ounce of my strength in order to stop you. You have to stay until we can get this whole thing sorted out."

Shaking loose from my iron-hard grasp like it was nothing more than the feeble grip of a bothersome child, his expression clouded over with menace. "I had thought to spare you," he snarled, "even though that plebeian you're with deserves to die for all the times he's thwarted my ambitions." Raising a glowing hand once more, he aimed it at us both. "But since you persist in being difficult, then I shall just have to kill you. I like this body; it suits me very well. *And I intend to keep it!*"

Jarrod cowered away, sobbing in fear, while I merely stared at the twisted spirit who'd once been my closest companion. "If that's the way it must be, then go ahead and do it!" I sneered, taking a calculated risk. "But I know Tunuhun is still alive in there, and he would never allow you to hurt us. He's much stronger than you give him credit for."

Ezra laughed, a bark of pure amusement that sent chills running down my spine. Then the light grew even stronger along Tunuhun's fingers, sizzling with imminent release, and I knew that this was the end.

Yet just before the spell was cast, his face twitched involuntarily, the muscles of his cheeks spasming as his eyes blinked in rapid succession. All along his stolen anatomy, a trembling erupted, the tremors causing his hands to quake while his eyelids continued to flutter. As the book dropped from his shaking fingers, the redness flowed back from his eyes, and then Tunuhun gazed out at us, restored to his former self before sliding bonelessly to the ground.

Rushing to his side, I checked his pulse by placing two fingers on his carotid artery. The heartbeat was strong, but irregular. As I attempted to straighten his limbs into a more comfortable position, his eyes cracked opened to peer back up at me.

"Sayaittuŋa," he whispered, his voice rusty.

"I know," I said. "You must be completely drained. Lie still a moment, rest, and then we'll get you out of here."

"Tuqutqayaq," he mumbled, his eyes sliding closed.

I was already well aware of how narrowly we'd just escaped death, but his reaffirmation of our close call hit me hard, nonetheless. What did we even think we were doing? We weren't heroes. We weren't militarily trained, or steeped in knowledge of the arcane or extraterrestrial. These threats to the planet, they were so much larger than us. Who were we to think that we could prevent them? And yet I knew that going to the authorities would only mean our incarceration or worse. They would never believe us, perhaps even think us mad, and we might even wind up in a mental facility, of no help to anyone. No, if these things happening now were to be stopped, it was up to us to gather more information and resources, to find others with similar talents who could possibly help us. We were the only ones in a position to unravel the mystery of what was going on around the globe and put a stop to it one way or another. If we left it up to others, it would already be too late. Staring down at my friend's battered face, I became even more resolved to doing whatever it took to defeat the evil rising all around us, no matter what else happened along the way.

"Come over here and help me with him," I said to Jarrod. "There has to be something that you can do, some spell or passage from the book you can use to restore him permanently."

Jarrod scooted closer, grabbing the fallen tome and dragging it over to him. "There ain't nothin I can do for him right this second," he said, riffling through the ancient pages of the unclean manuscript. "We need time to prepare."

"But back there, when you sent those rocks shooting out at Nathrotep, I saw that you have great power. Use it now to get that thing out of my friend!"

He snorted in derision, slamming the book closed. "That weren't nothin," he scoffed. "It is true that I do have some small amount of skill with all this here stuff, but it's infinitesimal when compared to what we been facin. The only reason why it worked at all was 'cause my grasp of the arts is so imperceptible that it didn't register with Nathrotep or any of his minions. It's the merest trickle of power when compared to what they was doin. No, for this here I need time to focus what little energy I have, perhaps even gain the assistance of someone with a much higher skill level than my own."

"Where do we find such a person?" I wondered aloud.

He thought a moment, sitting back on his haunches while cradling the book in his hands. "Well, your uncle done got this here book from some fellers down in South America. That there step pyramid we was on got me to thinking. Iffen we can find them other people, maybe mention your uncle's name, and show them this here book, well then, perhaps it might be we can get us some help."

"But how do we get there, and where exactly are those people located?"

"You leave that to me," he said, tucking the book into his rucksack and then slinging it across his broad back. "For now, let's just get him upright and then take him back to your car. We have to get outta here, and fast. There's no tellin what else will come crawlin outta the rest of them tunnels. Nathrotep and his filthy ghouls ain't the only things lurkin about under this here town."

I helped lift Tunuhun to his feet while I thought about what he'd said. It was as good a plan as any. We had to find some way to get the spirit out of Tunuhun as soon as possible and then discover where this map tile was leading us. Once we were able to locate other places around the globe which contained these ancient alien hives, then perhaps we'd find the means to stop the Mi-Go invasion as well as defeat the forces Nathrotep was preparing to bring against us. It was a long shot, but at least it was a start.

Between the two of us, we dragged Tunuhun out of the depths of the earth, stumbling across an overgrown graveyard as we headed back to where the car was parked. Morning sunlight filtered down on us, watery in the cold, predawn air, but we met no further resistance as we moved through the tumbled headstones. As we dragged Tunuhun over the moss-covered, ill-tended grounds of that ancient site, I thought about the destiny we were heading toward, a thing I could not foresee nor even guess at. Yet there was one thing that I was absolutely certain of:

We would meet this thing head-on and on our own terms. And I would let nothing stand in the way of our commitment to save the world from the threat of its almost certain destruction.

About the Author

William H. Nelson is the author of Nathrotep (2018), Within the Range of Reanimation (2020), and The Unnamed Town (2021). He grew up in Anchorage, Alaska where he attended college at UAA. During his time there, he was a regular contributor to several publications, including The  Radical (Radical Publications, 1992-94), The Auroran (Denali Publications 1993-96), and Rainsongs (Denali Publications 1995-96).

After moving to the Seattle area in 1998, he eventually met the love of his life, Lisa, and now lives with her and their cat Dipso, (named from the Greek word meaning 'thirsty'). William continues to write every day. In his spare time, he enjoys reading voraciously, playing the drums like a berserk spider-monkey, creating award-winning costumes and props for local conventions, watching movies with a passion bordering on obsession, and playing selections from his truly ginormous collection of epic fantasy board games.

Connect with William on Facebook!
www.facebook.com/williamhnelsonbooks